THE BOYFRIEND RULES OF GOOD BEHAVIOR

THE BOYFRIEND RULES OF GOOD BEHAVIOR

CATHERINE BATESON

HOLIDAY HOUSE / NEW YORK

First published 2005 by University of Queensland Press, Box
6042, St. Lucia, Queensland 4067 Australia as *Millie and the
Night Heron*
First published in the United States of America by Holiday
House, Inc. in 2006
Printed in the United States of America
www.holidayhouse.com
1 3 5 7 9 10 8 6 4 2

Library of Congress Cataloging-in-Publication Data
Bateson, Catherine, 1960–
[Millie and the night heron]
The boyfriend rules of good behavior / by Catherine Bateson.
p. cm.
Summary: Millie and her artist mother move away
from their best friends to a new town, where her mother
gets a proper job and a boyfriend, and Millie learns
to cope with all the changes.
ISBN-13: 978-0-8234-2026-1 (hardcover)
ISBN-10: 0-8234-2026-4 (hardcover)
[1. Single-parent families—Fiction. 2. Interpersonal relations—
Fiction. 3. Mothers and daughters—Fiction. 4. Identity—Fiction.
5. Diaries—Fiction. 6. Australia—Fiction.] I. Title.
PZ7.B3222Bo 2006
[Fic]—dc22
2006043393

Celebrating the Bateson–Chisholm–Kempton merger and with thanks to Hugh for listening and Helen-Sarah-and-Rachel for talking.

CHAPTER ONE

It started as a joke. Mum and Sheri were sitting around in the kitchen, our sitting-around room. The lounge room was the TV zone. Only Mitchell's dad sat in there—to discuss *parenting issues* with Sheri while Mum and I went for a long walk with Pavlov so we weren't in the way or, worse still, *influencing the decision making*. The kitchen was where all other decisions were made.

'I've finished my single-mother phase,' Sheri said. 'I have to find a man, Kate. This single life stinks. I don't know how you've coped for so long.'

'There's no one in this town,' Mum said calmly. She was cutting the sweet potato up faster than I could peel it. We were cooking dahl—that's an

Indian curry dish with lentils. Sheri's been a vegetarian since mad cow disease broke out in England. That was Patrick's fault. Patrick's my dad. Mum calls him the diva. He lives in England where mad cow disease was really bad.

'There are lots of people in this town,' I said, peeling my next sweet potato around and around, which is harder than just plain up and down.

'Not interesting, dynamic, sexy, arty men,' Mum said. 'And pick that up, will you, before Pavlov tries to eat it.'

'There must be,' Sheri said. 'The town's going ahead. Everyone says so. I think we should get out more, Kate. Go to things, meet people, schmooze around and get seen.'

'I'm not baby-sitting,' I told Sheri. 'Not more than one night a week and my rates have just gone up to eight dollars an hour.'

That was unfair, really, because Mitchell is quite good fun and as we all live together anyway, was it really babysitting? This is what Patrick would call an ethical question.

Sheri grinned. 'You're on, kid. And the first night is tomorrow, opening of the Not the Winter Blues Festival, cocktails first in the Town Hall. Katie, what are we going to wear?'

Sheri was one of those friends that teachers stop you sitting next to as soon as they work her out. She wasn't a good influence on anybody. The trouble with Sheri was that once she entered a phase she dragged everyone along with her. Her real name wasn't Sheri, it was Susan. But Sheri reckoned Susan didn't suit her in any phase, so she changed it. She did it legally, so even her mother had to remember to call her Sheri. She kept her own surname though. Mitchell's dad changed his when they had their commitment ceremony. Everyone thought that was pretty cool of Mitchell's dad. I thought it was wimpy.

So I should have known that Sheri would be like those sheriff heroes in the old movies, she'd get her man.

Out they sashayed the next night. It's a good word, isn't it—sashayed? We had to bring one new word to school every week and Ms McCarthy wrote them all on the board and then we'd write a poem or a small story using as many of them as we could manage. I took 'sashay' to school after Mum said, 'Look at us, Millie, sashaying off. Do we look fine or what?'

They always looked good, Sheri and Mum, in different ways. Sheri sewed stuff. She was a professional. She made wedding gowns, bridesmaids' dresses, mother-of-the-bride frocks and these cool cushions, bean bags and kid's clothes out of crazy fur fabric and old bedspreads. She sold them through local groovy shops in our area. She had a room at the back of the house which was entirely for her sewing things. She had baskets of material —she called it fabric—tins of buttons, buckles, embroidery threads, sari ribbons, beaded trims and all sorts of gorgeous things. She hardly ever bought clothes, even at the op shop. Sheri was curvy with big you-know-whats, curly hair, and brown eyes just like Pavlov, all warm and affectionate.

Mum, on the other hand, is less curvy, taller, grey-eyed, and her dark hair is frizzy. She dresses in browns rather than blacks—chestnut, chocolate and a deep eggplant purply-brown. That's her 'palette', she says. It makes it easy for her to go shopping. Then she has her painting clothes – old jeans or cords and Patrick's shirts. (He only wears white shirts and when they are a little worn at the cuffs he parcels them up and sends them to Mum to wear as painting smocks.)

Mum was wearing a new frock—eggplant brown with little rosebuds scattered all over it. It flowed around her. She wore new high-heel shoes, too. Mum's shoe collection is wild. Sheri sometimes said that that was where you could find Mum's soul— in the bottom of her wardrobe.

She passed on her shoe genes to me, but in a strange mutation they took over my whole dress sense. There is nothing of Mum's palette and Patrick's white shirts in me! I take after Sheri in that respect. Can you take after friend-relations? Sheri's been around since before I was born. She's practically related by blood.

Off they went, calling out instructions behind them. The usual stuff.

'If Simon rings, don't tell him where we are, just take a message.' (Simon is Mitchell's dad.)

'If Patrick rings, tell him I'm out man-hunting, and ask him about that project, too.'

'Do I have to say man-hunting? It's so gross.'

'Yes. Keep him in the loop, sweetie. It's good for him.'

Sheri stopped at the front gate and called out, 'You didn't wish us good luck or tell us how fantastic we look.'

'I don't know that I should wish you good luck,' I told her, following them up the path. 'Not for man-hunting. Isn't that illegal these days? Didn't they pass legislation in parliament?'

'That was duck-hunting,' Sheri said, laughing. 'Men are wilier and less endangered.'

'You both look good,' I said sincerely, 'and I love those shoes, Mum. Are they new?'

'On special,' Mum said, twisting her foot this way and that. 'I had to get them for the dress, Millie.'

'Just so long as you've paid my netball clinic?'

'Before I bought the shoes, Millie. Do I look like an irresponsible mother?'

'You look terrific,' I said. 'You too, Sheri. I like the cocktail leggings. Very sexy.'

'Oh Millie, you're a honey. I hope Mitchell takes after you when he's your age.'

'He won't,' I said. 'He's a boy, Sheri. They smell like dirty socks and old apples and they talk in a weird boy code.'

'The worst thing is,' Sheri said, 'they never change, baby. That's what they're like from your age onwards.'

'So why are you all dressed up and going man-hunting?'

Mum laughed. 'Good question. Sheri, do you want to lash out, buy a bottle of wine, rent a video and stay in?'

'No, I've made up my mind, Kate. I'm in my femme fatale flirt phase and no one and no rational argument is going to stop me.'

'Okay, let's keep on sashaying then,' Mum said.

I looked 'sashay' up later. I thought it might be the sound Mum's dress made as she swept up the path, but it means 'glide' or 'sway'.

Here are those week's words. I've put them in order of best to worst. I like doing that. Of course, this is just IMO, as Patrick writes in his emails:

SASHAY (mine)
INDIGO (Tom Fletcher. We were the
    brightest kids in our grade.)
COCHINEAL (Tessa.
    Actually, indigo and cochineal tie for second
best, but I'm writing the list so I chose Tom's
    over Tessa's because Tom's cool and Tessa
    teases me sometimes.)
CARTWHEEL (Frannie. I wouldn't have minded
    this being my word, actually.
            It was a good one.)
SOMERSAULT (Carina. I think Frannie might
    have whispered it to her. Carina's sweet
    but not that bright.)
SACRED (Sarah. Every one of her words
        is religious. It is a phase she
            is going through.)
JANGLE (Penny. Ms McCarthy was keen on
    sound words and once Penny got the hang
        of them, she did one every week. She
    had a crush on Ms McCarthy.)
LUNAR (Nicole, the new girl.)
BRUISED (Peter M. He always goes for
        injuries. He's on the soccer team.)
PASSIONATE (Tracey. She said it and then
    blushed. She's in love with ...)
    ELBOW (boring Jeremy, aka Jazza,
who always says body parts because he can't

think of anything better. Mind you,
    they come in handy, as you'll see.)
DEATH
SKULL (Mark, Morrison and David.)
PLAGUE
TREBUCHET (Alasdair. It's a medieval war
  thingy, not a catapult. He was very clear
  about that but I never did find out what it
    actually was. I couldn't use it anyway.)
MAHOGANY (Daniel, the undertaker's son.)
HARMONY (Honey McPherson.
    Her mum teaches yoga.)
OATH (Travis. He's into medieval war as well.)
CHIVALROUS (Peter B. Plays with Travis
  and Alasdair, obviously. They were building a
  trebuchet together to fire tennis balls.
    But it is not a catapult.)

The other words were too boring to be recorded.
This is my poem from that week.

Kate and Sheri sashayed out in
cochineal and indigo while the lunar sky
cartwheeled and somersaulted
just for their jangling glory.

Here is an oath for Sheri's passionate
elbow - no death, no plague but

chivalrous sacred harmony follow those two
on their heart's journey.

Sheri liked the poem so much she made me
print her out a copy which she put in her journal
under the day's date. Mum stuck her copy up on
her studio wall.

They got home just as the late, late movie
started. It was some kind of horror remake and I
wasn't that keen on watching it, but I had a baby-
sitting rule that I could watch television until they
got home, so I would have had to watch either it
or some doco on SBS about Africa, which looked
just as horrifying, but in a more real way.

'How did it go?'

'Pretty good,' Sheri said, waving a business
card at me. 'Not bad for our first time, eh Kate?'

'The cocktails were good,' Mum said, hugging
me good night, 'and Sheri chatted up a bloke.'

The bloke rang a couple of days later. I wrote
his name and number down on the phone board.
Brendan Trotter, he said his name was, then
spelled it out to me as though I couldn't spell, and
made me repeat his phone number to make sure
I'd got it right. I didn't like him from the beginning.

CHAPTER TWO

Mum didn't like him either. One day he was kidding around in the kitchen and wrote down a shopping list for each of us.

'What do you want?' he asked Mitchell. 'What do you need to make your life complete?'

'A scooter,' Mitchell said without thinking. 'A proper one, like Dylan's got.'

'And you, Millie?'

The world was so full of things I needed to make my life complete, I couldn't think. There was the Gotcha Girls latest CD, sunglasses would be cool, the next book in the *Lady of Glenfair* trilogy, a pair of knee-high boots. My head spun with choices.

'We'll come back to you, then,' he said. 'Kate?'

'I don't want anything,' Mum said.

'Come on, Kate,' he wheedled. I think he knew she didn't like him and he wanted her to.

'I have everything,' Mum said firmly. 'I have Millie, Mitchell and Sheri, a studio – what else could I need?'

'You're a hard woman, Kate. Sheri – no, I know what you want.' And he wrote *love, care and attention* down on the shopping list, while Sheri kissed him and Mitchell and I made being-sick noises, but quietly.

'I want toe socks,' I said suddenly. 'Toe socks and the next book in the *Lady of Glenfair* series.'

'How come she gets two things?' Mitchell objected.

'Because she's a girl, Mitch,' Brendan said, 'and girls always want more than men want.'

'That's not true,' Mum said, bristling.

'Not women like Kate,' Brendan said smoothly, 'but girls do.'

'I'll settle for the book,' I said quickly, and watched him write it down.

It seemed hardly any time before Sheri and Mitchell moved out to live with Brendan. Sheri said that when you know something's right, you go for it. She had been alone for too long, she said, and so had Brendan. He was responsible, loving, a professional man (he was the local school counsellor) and they shared a love of jazz, movies and good food.

Mum said it didn't bother her that it had happened fast. It was just something about him.

Sheri said, 'You just don't want us to move. You're locked in a co-dependent relationship with me, Kate. You've been depending on me for your social life for the last five years, ever since Patrick went away. You need to get out more. You need to see more people. You need to like your own company more, learn to enjoy being alone.'

'What's this co-dependent relationship stuff? Where did you get all this psycho-babble from?' Mum asked. 'Brendan? It sounds just like the kind of stuff he says.'

'Well, he did say it would be hard for you when I move.'

It was more than hard. It was totally different. I'd get home from school, thump my bag down, wander into the kitchen looking for food and there would be no one there. Sheri used to always be in the kitchen when Mitchell and I got home from school. She'd make us toast or juice or hot chocolate. She'd ask about our day, chat about hers. I'd do my homework in the back sewing room if Sheri had the radio on. She didn't mind if I chatted to her while she worked. You can't often talk to Mum when she's working. Art is just different. You have to concentrate more. Craft, which is what Sheri did, is more user-friendly IMO. (IMO means 'in my opinion'. Patrick and I use it in emails all the time.)

We didn't have house meetings any more. What was the point with just the two of us? We didn't have group Saturday clean-ups. Mum would clean up any old time — and suddenly, swooping down like Genghis Kahn on the barbarians. We didn't have big curry cook-ups, or crazy dancing in the kitchen, or girls' nights in with face-masks, hair dyeing, make-your-own-pizza and a tear-jerker video. Mum worked all hours in the studio. She wore old jeans and Patrick's shirts for weeks on end. She wore her paint-spattered sandshoes while her soul gathered dust in the bottom of the wardrobe.

I called the house meeting. I sent Mum an invitation. I'm not good at art, not like Mum, so I did a collage. There was a picture of a pizza, a musical note, a champagne glass and then the words:

You are invited to a pizza-and-music
  house meeting.
This is because Millie, your daughter,
  misses you.

Please dress up appropriately -
your rosebud dress and cherry-coloured
Mary Janes would be suitable.
7.00 pm sharp on Friday night.
RSVP by 3.30 pm.

I left it propped up on her easel where she couldn't miss it.

When I got home from school there was a note stuck on my door.

Millie,
Thank you for your invitation. I will be there with bells on. I've bought pizza makings, cranberry juice (your favourite), and there's a new top on your bed you might like to wear. I saw it this morning at the op shop and thought of you. I look forward to tonight. Give me a buzz at the studio when you get home.
Lots of love
Mum xxxxx

I didn't buzz her straightaway. I was expecting an email from Patrick. Sure enough, there it was:

```
> To: milliethegreatest@mail.com
> From: pmcd@lndonuni.edu.uk
>
```

14.

```
> Millie my sweet,
> Change is needed. Sheri is right.
> Your mother needs CHANGE in her life.
> She should get out in the world more.
> I hope you're not feeling DEPRESSED
> about all this, Millie. Don't become
> one of those American girls on ANTI-
> DEPRESSANTS, for heaven's sake. Life
> is GOOD.
>
> I think you both should MOVE, meet
> NEW people, start a NEW life. Give
> your mother a HUG from me. She is one
> of my FAVOURITE people in the world
> and I MISS her. You are my MOST
> FAVOURITE. That goes without saying.
>
> LOTS OF LOVE
> patrick.
> -----------------------------------
```

It was a typical Patrick email. He wrote emails the way he talked.

'So,' Mum said later, eating pizza, 'what's on the house meeting agenda?' She was wearing her rosebud dress and she'd clipped a flower in her hair. I was wearing my denim skirt with the new top, which was very groovy. It had a picture of an

Indian goddess on it and the front of it was my favourite colour—a greeny blue, a little like the ocean.

'I miss you,' I said. 'You're not like you used to be when Sheri lived with us.'

'I've been working,' Mum said. 'I thought if I really got stuck into work, I'd feel better, you know?'

'And do you?'

'Well, sort of,' Mum said, 'but not entirely. I miss Sheri, but I think it's more than that. I feel there's a hole in my life. I haven't just been working. I've been re-assessing and I've applied for a job.'

'You've got a job,' I said. 'You make art.'

'I'll always make art, but making art isn't enough for me. I need a job. I need to get out more. I think we need to move. A bigger place. Somewhere with a proper gallery. I don't want to move back to the city, it's too expensive. But I want a change of scenery.'

'But I like this scenery,' I said. 'I like where we live. I like this town.'

'It's all going to be different for you next year, anyway,' Mum said calmly.

I couldn't see how she could go on just eating her pizza like that as though everything was okay. My mouth felt all dry and my stomach was wobbling. I could hardly eat another piece. I ate it anyway. It was Kate-and-Millie's Special with extra cheese and extra olives.

'So what's the job?'

'Head of the Art Department at Wetlands TAFE.'

'Where's that?'

'About 150 kilometres down the coastline,' Mum said, 'I thought we'd go and have a look next weekend. My interview is Monday week. I gather they are pretty desperate for someone to take over.'

'Take over?'

'The Art Department, darling. Just think, if I get the job I'll be head of the Art Department.'

'What about me?' I wailed. 'What about this house? What about school next year? What about Frannie and Carina? They're my best friends in the world and I won't ever see them again. Have you even thought of me?'

'Yes,' Mum said, glaring at me, 'of course I have. Millie, it's going to be hard for you, I know that. But you will make new friends. You have a huge capacity for friendship. And think, Sweetie, Frannie is going to Our Lady's next year and Carina is moving back to the city. You know that.'

'I could still see them,' I whined.

'You can still see them when, *if* we move. Think

of having real money. Think of exploring a new place. Anyway, Millie, I haven't even got the job yet. I think I'm a good artist, and I am a good art teacher, but I have never been head of any department, so I probably won't get a look in.'

I hardly slept all that night. Mum said it was a mixture of indigestion and watching *Buffy* too late at night, but it was really the idea of moving. I hated it.

CHAPTER THREE

We stayed at a Bed and Breakfast, with views, the brochure read, of spectacular mountain ranges on one side and the sea on the other. The mountain ranges had been cleared by loggers and the sea wasn't visible at all. The B & B also promised a 'delicious five-star breakfast' which turned out to be a loaf of Tip Top raisin bread — toaster provided — a tin of fruit salad in light syrup, four rashers of bacon and two eggs.

'Free range eggs,' Mum said.

'I can see that,' I told her, washing chicken poop off mine. 'I like them better when they come out of a carton.'

'Oh, you do not, Millie. If you did, you'd never

have written that letter to the local paper about how bad it was to keep battery hens. You told me you were an animal rights activist.'

'I am,' I said, 'but I prefer my eggs without farm life evidence. Does that look clean to you?'

'Good enough to eat,' Mum said, and swooped down on me, hugging me tight and nearly breaking my egg. 'I love you, Millie girl, even if you are a cantankerous kid.'

Mum got high on new places. I'd forgotten that. It had been a long time between real holidays, because we often didn't have quite enough money around holiday time when everything, even petrol, went up.

Gradually I caught Mum's enthusiasm. It took a mixture of food, shopping and walking. In that order, of course. The best food was provided by the hospitality students of Wetlands TAFE at their restaurant, *The Pelicano*. They had children's rates, but the waiting staff treated me just as seriously as they treated Mum. They read the Specials board and didn't mind when I asked whether the duck was free range.

Rebecca — we knew that was her name because she introduced herself to us — agreed with me that they should be using free range ducks but they didn't because of the expense. She also said that in her opinion they should widen the vegetarian choices, but it didn't worry us because Sheri wasn't there.

'If I get this job,' Mum said, as we drove back to the B & B, bellies full of Rack of Lamb encrusted with Honey Mustard and served on a Bed of Mash, 'and I do say *if*, Sweetie, because I really don't have the qualifications, but if I get this job, we could make that our treat restaurant.'

The Red Cross Op-Shop was the best. It didn't have that op shop smell, even, and for once there were young people working there. Not that I'm against old ladies in op shops, but I think it's pretty cool to walk into an op shop where the radio is tuned to FM and there's an essential-oil burner on the counter. The clothes were fantastic. It was like shopping at a boutique. We only spent twenty dollars and I walked out with a new summer outfit.

The walk was over the wetlands themselves. There were hides where you could sit and watch the birds without them seeing you: pelicans, ducks, little blue-feathered moor hens. It was very peaceful. You had to be very quiet and I leant against Mum's shoulder while we both watched the groups of pelicans sailing grandly past. She put her arm around me and we stayed like that for the longest time, just sitting close, not saying anything, the bird noises like music someone had forgotten to turn off.

Eventually Mum kind of shook herself, the way you do when you've been daydreaming and suddenly realise that the toast has burnt.

'Oh, Millie,' she said, 'I wish I could paint us the way we are now. I wish I could do that.'

'You could, Mum. You can paint anything.'

'No.' She sighed. 'Figures in landscape aren't in my vocabulary.'

'Can't you add to it? You're always telling me to broaden my vocabulary.'

'That's words, darling. You should always use more and different words.'

'Why shouldn't you do the same with painting?' I hated it when adults told you one thing and then told themselves something completely opposite. Why did they do that? There was a long silence. Not quite silence, of course, because all the birds were calling out to each other and squabbling over little fish.

'You might be right, Millie,' Mum said slowly. 'Maybe I should. It's just scary stepping out from what you know you can do and trying something different, something that mightn't work.'

'But you're doing that now,' I argued. Sometimes Mum was peculiarly stupid for an intelligent woman. 'I mean, going for this job. How do you know that's going to work, but you've sailed into that, haven't you? And you're always telling me not to be scared of life.'

Mum laughed. I liked it when she laughed. It was such a glad sound, as though the sun had brightened all of a sudden.

'Oh, Millie, you're a wise child,' she said, hugging me hard to her side, awkwardly, because she was doing it with only the arm that was still around me.

'And a wild one,' I said, pleased. 'Don't forget that I'm a wild girl.'

I sat in the car while she went for her job interview. She got dressed up, in an artist-goes-for-a-job kind of way. We both wished Sheri had been there. Mum had brought every last respectable thing with her, of course, which was fine, but none of them went with each other.

'These trousers,' I said, holding up a pair. They were my favourite. They looked liked old men's trousers — you know, brown checks — but groovy, too.

'Brown's not a power colour, darling,' Mum said. 'Damn. I wish I was like your father. He'd just throw on one of his eternal white shirts, a pair of dark trousers and an unusual, look-at-me-I'm-a-genius tie and get the damn job before he'd opened his mouth.'

'Well, you're not Patrick.'

There is always someone practical in a family, isn't there? Someone who has to state the plain truth in an in-your-face way so that everyone stops dreaming about what might be and gets on with the life in front of them. I was that person.

Eventually Mum wore a different pair of trousers, my second favourite pair, the colour of dark chocolate, and with that a pale pink shirt and a dark scarf draped in an arty way and secured with a kilt pin. She let her hair go wild. There wasn't much else she could do — it was going to rain.

I waited in the car and it did rain. Lashings of water streamed down the front window and the trees bent so far over I thought some of the smaller ones would snap. Mum was gone forever, leaving me lots of time to think. Have you noticed how thoughts come in little gasps and how each one leads to another? But if you said to someone, I started out thinking about pelicans and ended up thinking about pizza, you'd be the only person probably in the world who would know how pelicans could lead you to thinking of pizza napolitana as made by D'Angelos. Not that I was thinking of pelicans. That's just an example.

I actually thought:

1. Do trees ever snap in the rain?
2. Does our boot still leak and is there anything of mine in it?
3. If Mum gets this job, will she get a new car?
4. It'd be cool to have a car with a CD.
5. I wouldn't mind being a famous singer.
6. But I can't sing in tune.
7. I don't want to be a scientist, I can never spell what Patrick is doing.
8. An artist would be okay, except that's what Mum is, so it's been taken.
9. Can you be struck by lightning if you're in a car?
10. That's a Patrick question.
11. Maybe being a scientist isn't a bad idea.
12. But I might have to go overseas.
13. I would be a lawyer.
14. Was that more lightning?
15. I should join a debating society if I'm going to be a lawyer.
16. I wonder whether there will be one at my new school.
17. I don't want to move.
18. But I don't want to stay living the way we are either.
19. I wish Sheri had never met Brendan Trotter.
20. What kind of name is that anyway?

21. If I was called Brendan Trotter, I'd change my name, first thing.
22. That was lightning.
23. If I wasn't a Millie I wouldn't mind being a Phoebe.
24. I met a dog once called Phoebe. It's a name wasted on a dog.
25. Cute dog, though - a West Highland Terrier.

See what I mean — from trees and rain to West Highland Terriers in twenty-five thoughts.

I'd just added them up when Mum came out, running to the car, holding the portfolio of photographs close to her to protect it from the rain. I lent over and opened the door for her.

'How did it go?'

She slammed the door shut and chucked the folder on to the back seat. Her hair was all wet and the curls lay flat, but as soon as the car heater went on, it would begin to frizz in all directions.

'I don't know,' she said. She sounded kind of sad and flat.

'What do you mean, you don't know?' That was what she always said to me. 'You must have some idea.'

Mum shrugged and turned the ignition key. The car started first time. It didn't always do that.

26.

It must have sensed her mood.

'I just don't know. They said they needed someone pretty soon, and asked whether I could move in that time, and I said, yes, of course, but they also said I hadn't had any experience in that role and was I sure the administration side of things wouldn't be too much. I just don't know, Millie. You know how it is when you finish a test. You hope you've done well, but you don't know.'

'Well, if you don't get it, they don't know what they've missed. I know you could do the job perfectly, Mum.'

She smiled at me but it wasn't her big smile. It was her little, weak-around-the-edges one, like when Patrick forgets her birthday — which he does sometimes, although he always tries to make up for it later.

It isn't that she and Patrick love each other in that 'lurve' way — you know, smooching and Valentine's Day cards and how Sheri and Brendan carried on. It's that they are each other's best friend. They had been forever and then they decided to try to be more than that, and that's when they had me. But it didn't work, Mum said, because they were too used to each other.

'I don't know, Millie. Maybe it *would* be too much for me. I haven't that kind of experience. I don't even know that I can still teach art. I haven't done it for years and I don't think I did a good job then.'

'Mum!' I hated it when she got in these moods. 'Stop being a pestimist.'

That's a family joke. Mitchell used to say 'pestimist' instead of 'pessimist', when he was little.

'Oh, Millie, I'm sorry. It's just that when I walked in ... It wasn't like a proper interview. It was kind of all cosy. They were just sitting around their staff room, chatting. There was real coffee brewing. I could smell it before the door opened. I thought, I could like these people. I could like working here.'

We drove back to town in silence except for the odd sniffle from Mum. I was worried about her crying and driving at the same time, but there was so much rain outside I supposed a bit inside couldn't hurt.

We found a café and Mum went to the Ladies to check that her mascara hadn't run. When she came out, she looked a little better.

'Can't do anything about it,' she said, over the menu. 'Either I get it or I don't. We'll have to leave it up to Fate and Destiny, Millie. I'll tell you what, let's call in on Sheri and Mitchell on the way home?'

'We had dinner at this restaurant called *The*

Pelicano,' I told Mitchell. We were in the rumpus room while Sheri and Mum had a good talk in the kitchen. 'There was a statue of pelicans, a really good one, and a girl called Rebecca served us. The food was awesome.'

'I want to live with you again, Millmill,' Mitchell said, sitting closer, 'I don't like it here much.'

'What's wrong, Mitchell? I thought you were happy.'

'I was, sort of. We never do anything. Not together, the way we all used to. He shouts, too, when you don't think you've done anything really bad. He shouts.'

'Oh, Mitchell, you know how people get stressed. Maybe he's just stressed. He listens to people's problems all day, after all.'

'It's okay when he's not here,' Mitch said. 'I like it then. The TV is really big. Did you see it? But I can't watch it that much.'

We didn't stay long because Sheri had to cook dinner and we were not invited to stay.

'He's under pressure,' I heard her say. 'Sometimes he doesn't come home until nearly midnight, but he rang today and said he'd be home for dinner. I hope you understand, Kate.'

'Of course,' Mum said and we both gave Sheri a big hug.

Our house looked too big when we got home. Mum looked at me and we both put our shoes back on and went out for dinner. Mum had a glass of wine and I had a coke spider.

Most of the streetlights in our street were out when we walked home later and the sky was full of stars.

Mum said, 'What can you see?'

'The Southern Cross,' I said. 'Look, there are the two pointers. But I don't know the other names. I keep forgetting.'

'I think I can see the Pleiades,' Mum said, pointing to a hazy bit of sky, 'but I always just think I can see them. I'm never sure. Imagine, Millie, whether we are here looking at them or not, those stars keep on shining. That's something, isn't it?'

I wasn't sure if that was such a cheerful thought, but I kept that to myself.

CHAPTER FOUR

Mum didn't get the Head of the Art Department job. Instead she was asked to be a tutor with the Art Department, teaching Life Drawing, Colour and Composition, and Art and Industry. She took the job without even asking me.

'It's not as much money, Millie,' she said, 'but it's a job. They said they were excited about getting someone with my talent. Oh, Millie, it's a great opportunity for me.'

I walked around our house that afternoon trying to work out what I would miss. It was, after all, just a house. I'd miss my hiding place under the front stairs where I kept a candle, a box of matches and a packet of dried fruit — except mice had eaten the dried fruit.

I walked around our town. I'd outgrown the playground but I would miss the river and the river walks. In the end, though, it was just a town like any other.

'Okay,' I said when I got home just as the sun was going down, 'when do we start packing?'

'We have to find a place first, and there's Christmas,' Mum said. 'We have to give notice here. Oh, poor Mrs Hetherington. Still, she should find someone else. This is a good house and the rent's reasonable.'

We spent Christmas Day with Sheri and Mitchell. We had for as many Christmases back that I could remember. Usually Simon joined us, and sometimes Patrick if he was in the country. But this year Simon couldn't come because Brendan didn't want him, and Patrick was stuck in London, though he sent me a beautiful teddy bear. It had a hand-knitted jumper on and was softer than any other teddy bear I owned. I know I should have outgrown teddy bears, but it's okay to have very special ones. He sent Mum some earrings he'd bought on a holiday in Italy and a new CD of some jazzy, bluesy music he knew she'd like. He sent her a hefty cheque, too, to help with the move.

Patrick had more money than we had, but

living in London was expensive. Sometimes he gets extra money, when he has a scientific paper published in America or is asked to lecture somewhere, and then he always sends us something.

The truth is that I was an accident. Patrick didn't really want a child at all. He wanted to be a scientist and he knew he shouldn't have children until he was at least forty years old, which isn't old for a man to have children. But then Mum got pregnant and she'd wanted a little girl since *she* was a little girl so she told Patrick she'd look after me whether he did or not. Of course, when I was born, Patrick loved me completely, because babies are just like that. But he still loved science too.

I know I should want a dad like most other people have, but I don't know. I have Patrick and he's like this friend *and* a dad. But he wasn't there on Christmas Day and we missed him.

We wouldn't have missed him so much if it had been a normal Christmas Day with Sheri and Mum drinking a little too much champagne and talking about the stuff they always talked about, like:

1. Food you shouldn't order on a first date (spaghetti anything, noodles anything, anything with raw onion - in case he

decided to kiss you - garlic bread - ditto - or curry laksa - you always splash it on your good clothes).

2. Men they've fallen for, why and why they fell out of love.

3. My favourite - what they'd do if they won Tattslotto. And there's to be no cheating. You have to really believe you've won it and make good decisions and know exactly what you want. You get points if you can say, 'I want a poodle pink handbag, like the one Tessa was showing off at school. You get them from Run Dog Run and they cost $25.95.'

And best of all, we play Cosmic Encounters, the only board game Sheri and Mum will play.

But we didn't do anything like that and I knew it was because Brendan was there.

Sheri had done a proper turkey, with some weird chestnut stuffing. We never have turkey. We have fish, sausages, kebabs and tofu, cooked on the barbeque, under cover if it is wet or windy. She'd made some strange cake, too. She called it a stained glass window cake and it was beautiful — to look at. We never have that kind of cake. We have Mum's ice-cream-filled panettone, which is an Italian Christmas cake. Sometimes we mix up toffee into the ice-cream and it's all cold and soft with the odd crunch. Sheri's cake had too many of those green and red cherries in it. Mitchell and I hate those cherries.

It was all kind of rushed, too, which Christmas Day never is. It is always the longest day in the year. But almost as soon as we arrived, Brendan had us sitting down eating. We had hardly properly thanked anyone for their presents. And you know how the presents have to be done. First of all you have to open the card, read it and then you have to open the present, slowly if you can so as not to tear the paper, and then you look at the present and exclaim and then you have to thank the person with a kiss and say something absolutely right about the present.

So, if it's a top in your favourite colour, you have to say, 'Oh wow! Sheri, purple's my favourite colour and this will go perfectly with my almost-new black jeans we bought at the op shop only last week and my purple shell bangle. I think I'll wear it all to this year's school disco. Thank you soooo much, Sheri. You always buy the best clothes!'

It's easy to do that with Sheri–Mum–Patrick presents, but it is harder to do with presents you don't much like. But you have to give it a go, because it is Christmas and that's what you have to do at Christmastime.

35.

I expected Brendan's present to be the latest book in the *Lady of Glenfair* series, because he knew I wanted that and you always give someone the present you think is exactly right and the one you honestly believe *they will simply love*. I had my mouth open to say, 'Wow! Brendan, thank you so much. I've been wanting this book for ages.'

Brendan's book was *12 Steps for Successful Teens*.

'I think you'll find that very useful,' he said. 'It's a book I recommend to my clients.'

Fortunately Mum had taught me what to say under those circumstances. I looked at Brendan and said, 'Thank you, Brendan. It's very thoughtful.'

Inside I was fuming. Clients. He recommended it to his *clients*. Brendan's clients are troubled teenagers. They have problems. They have big problems, if you believed Brendan. He gave Mum a book, too — *12 Steps for Raising Successful Teens*.

'Do you get a professional discount on these?' Mum asked in her too-sweet voice. 'Sheri, are you going to open the champagne I bought?' She didn't say thank you until her glass was full. I could see Sheri making pleading, be-nice-please faces at her. 'Thanks Brendan. I'm sure it will be useful.'

Then Brendan bustled us to the table, saying

we could open the other presents there. Which we did, but Sheri wasn't even there. She was in the kitchen, dishing up the turkey. So we couldn't thank anyone properly and Mitchell was oddly quiet and Brendan was the only one really talking. He was just going on and on and on about rituals in the modern world, how we'd lost them, and I wanted to stand up and shout, well, you've changed all ours, you boring old man. But I couldn't, because Sheri was looking strained and pale and Mum was determinedly smiling and smiling.

It was the worst Christmas Day.

Brendan left straight after lunch.

'A family in need,' he said mysteriously, collecting some parcels from under the Christmas tree. 'I'll be back later.' And he vanished.

'He sees these families,' Sheri said after we'd all heard his car back out of the driveway and drive off. 'He's very responsible. Really. He's the most selfless man I've ever met.'

It didn't get better without him. Mum and Sheri shut themselves into the kitchen with the rest of the champagne and told Mitchell and me to go and play.

'Did you get your scooter?' I asked Mitchell, while we hit a few balls around the snooker table downstairs.

'Nuh.' Mitchell potted the black. If Mitchell would only go for the right balls, he'd be a good player. He seemed too depressed to care.

'What did you get?'

'From him? A book called *Boys: 12 Steps to Loving Yourselves*. I don't understand it. He could have got me a Paul Jennings book. Something I want to read. Mum said she'd get me a scooter soon. She just couldn't afford it yet. We pay more rent here than we did when we lived with you, she said, and the food is more expensive.'

'You pay rent here?'

'Well, sort of. I don't get it, Millie. I just want to live with you guys.'

We left before Brendan could get back.

I wasn't going to sit through another Christmas like that. I was pleased we were moving.

'Next Christmas,' I said to Mum, to cheer her up, because she was driving home with the grimmest look on her face, 'we'll be in our new house in a new town with new friends.'

'I'm worried about Sheri,' Mum said. 'She's changing, isn't she, Millie? She even looks paler — everything about her, I mean.'

I knew what she was talking about – no bright purple tights, no dark plum tints in her hair, no tie-dyed t-shirt. Sheri had been dressed in a long pale skirt and her hair had been pulled back tightly into a little pony tail. She looked like someone else.

'Maybe we shouldn't leave while she's like this. She might need us,' Mum said.

'She left us, Mum. We didn't leave her. And what about your job?' Suddenly I wanted to be out of this town. I had said goodbye to it in my mind. I didn't want another awful Christmas Day.

'You're right, Millie. The job really has to come first. What it will be like to have some money! I'll be able to have an exhibition. That's the first thing I'm going to do, Millie. Organise an exhibition.'

That's the funny thing with art. You have to have money in order to make it. You have to even have money so you can sell it. Then you have an exhibition and if you don't sell anything, you've spent money trying to make money and you're further in debt. I tell you, I'm going to be a lawyer. First thing at my new school, I'm signing up for the debating society. That's how you start being a lawyer. I saw it on TV.

When I make lots of money as a lawyer, everyone can come to my Christmas Days and I will buy everyone the presents I know they'll love.

Mum's present was awesome. It always is. And my present to her was pretty good, too. I bought her three sketchbooks in different sizes. One for her purse, so she could make sketches on the run, a bigger one and then a really big one. I'd saved up for them for weeks and I wrote on the biggest one in my best handwriting:

For Kate Childes
so she can enlarge her artistic vocabulary,
from her loving daughter, Millie,
with best wishes for our new life

So we had to move to make sense of my Christmas present.

Later that night I wrote what I got for Christmas in my journal. I do that every year.

1. Mum's present - a brand new book of a brand new series by one of my favourite writers, a new purple denim skirt, a pair of rainbow toe socks, a little bag filled with hair thingies, and bath oil with glitter, which I'd better use quickly in case our new house doesn't have a bath.
2. Sheri - a CD voucher and a groovy little black velvet bag covered with buttons and with my initials embroidered on it.
3. Patrick - the teddy bear I have named Merlin.

4. Patrick's sister-who-lives-in-Toronto, Bridie - a gorgeous card and a book on Easy Knitting Projects for the Beginner. I think I must have told her in an email that I wanted to learn to knit. And I do.
5. Patrick's Mum, my grandmother, although I call her May - $50! And a card telling me to spend it on 'frippery'. I had to look that up in the dictionary.
6. Mitchell - a pack of UNO cards, which was great because I think we lost some from our other pack, and a travelling chess set. I can't actually play chess yet, but this, as I told him, is a good incentive to learn.
7. Brendan - well, you know that already

Usually you just get over Christmas and there is New Year's Eve, but this year on New Year's Eve Mum and I just went down and watched the fireworks on the oval and Mum gave me a sip of champagne and we told each other we loved each other best in the entire world, toasted to our new life and went to bed.

When we woke up, it was a brand new year and it had rained, so it looked shiny and new, just the kind of day I like best.

CHAPTER FIVE

The house I wanted was a big old rambling one with the kind of windows you read about in really old books, the kind imprisoned lovers carve their names on with a diamond ring, or a lonely sickly child sits at, watching the rain fall and dreaming of her father, lost at sea.

It wasn't even up for rent. We rented the little house up the road from it.

Our house had carpet older than I was, a thin peppering of mould across one of the entrance room walls and all the windows were locked, but not with keys, with lengths of dowel specially cut to fit.

'We'll do things,' Mum said. 'We'll get it right,

Millie, and look at the back yard. There's a vegie garden.'

'So?'

'So tomatoes, lettuces, fresh herbs, silver beet, bok choy — we'll practically be able to live from that vegie garden. And you'll be able to bicycle to school.'

'When it rains?'

It wasn't that I didn't like the house. Okay, so I didn't like the house, but I was also nervous. I'd looked at the school. It looked old. It looked old and big and grim. I was used to the school in our old town. It had stopped looking so big. Frannie and I used to ride our bikes down the steep concrete path on the weekend. We used to hide out near the canteen and play mafia gangsters. This new school looked mean — and that's when it was empty. What would it be like with hundreds of feral kids scattered around the grounds?

'Maybe I can drive you or you can put a rain jacket on and walk. Maybe you'll find a friend who lives near by and you can walk together. That's what I used to do. On the first day of school, everyone will be new. You'll have nothing to worry about.'

Mum was wrong. On the first day of school all the girls in my class who looked at all interesting — and I don't mean just pretty or popular but interesting – did know each other. There were three of them and they went around as Helen-Sarah-and-Rachel without a breath between their names. They were the girls I wanted to be with.

'Why?' Mum asked when I got home.

'One of them had the *Lady of Glenfair*, Book One, in her bag. She'd got it for Christmas. She said she was going to design herself a dress like the Fair Lady wears to her awful sister's wedding. That was Helen, I think. She's the middle one. The tallest is Rachel and she's the sweet one. The shortest is Sarah and she's mad about vampires. They are the only girls in my grade worth talking to. The others are just bland. Oh, and I'm a singleton. That's a student who doesn't come from one of the schools around here. How awful is that? Labelled a *singleton* from day one.'

'A singleton? That's kind of weird, isn't it? Oh, I suppose as in single rather than a group of kids?'

'I know what it means, Mum. I'm not totally stupid!'

'Sorry, Millie, of course you do. Give yourself some time. You always rush at everything. You won't be a singleton forever, you'll be a …'

'See! They don't even have a proper name if you're part of a group. Once you're a singleton you're always a singleton.'

It was true. I waited for two weeks and nothing happened to change my opinion. The bland girls talked about boys, clothes — but in a boring brand-names way — boys, netball, boys, popstars — usually boys — and TV shows.

I signed up for the Debating Society and who else signed up? Helen-Sarah-and-Rachel. We were the only girls from our grade to put our names down.

'Not enough to make a team,' the teacher in charge said, sighing, 'but we might be able to give you a taste of what it's like later in the year. Okay, girls?'

That was typical. If there hadn't been so many bland girls we might have had a chance.

'School would be like this wherever we lived,' Mum said. She had started teaching and the TAFE was letting her use a studio over there, as well, for herself. Every day when I went to school, she started the old beast (that's our car – it used to belong to Patrick's mum before they said she couldn't drive because of her eyesight) and drove off to paint or teach at the TAFE. Every afternoon she came home around the same time as me, or sometimes a little later. She didn't just come home, she bounced, like Tigger.

Her enthusiasm depressed me.

'You're absolutely right about enlarging my vocabulary,' she said, 'and my students are helping. They are so wonderful, Millie, such talent and such dedication. It's a privilege to teach them. I hope you'll be like that when you find something you really want to do when you leave school. It makes my job easy. You know, I wake up in the morning and can't believe they're paying me to do this.'

'They'd better pay you. We've got this school camp coming up, Mum, and it costs the earth.'

'Oh Millie, it sounds exciting,' Mum said, reading the notice. 'And what a good idea to have a camp so soon in the school year. It'll be a bonding experience.'

'As if we're all some kind of glue and have to stick to each other. You sound like Brendan.'

The truth was, I was dreading the camp, absolutely dreading it. The idea of being in a dormitory with all those girls, having to get into my pyjamas in front of them, clean my teeth next to them, and eat breakfast in front of everyone, didn't thrill me the slightest little bit. I was plotting severe sudden illness, like, oops Mum, it's bubonic plague.

You see, other kids scare me. I don't know what to talk to them about. I'm too weird. It's not so bad with kids I've known forever. At my old school with Frannie, most of the time we were sworn blood sisters, except for when she played with Tessa. We slept over at each other's places and we invited each other to our birthdays and it was fine. For a whole year we were witches together. That's because Frannie is nearly as weird as I am.

Sheri said I shouldn't say 'weird'. I should say 'individualistic' and 'opinionated'. She said that one day I would come into my own and then the world had better watch out. Sheri used to say things like that until she met Brendan.

Brendan said, 'That's a troubled child. There'll be problems ahead there, I can see them now.' I heard him. I was hiding in the broom cupboard at the time. It's a long story, but I wouldn't mind betting he knew I was there, because I saw him through the little crack and he gave the cupboard a long, suspicious stare as though he did know and he meant me to hear what he said.

Some days I thought the old Sheri was right and other days I thought Brendan might be right. Mum simply didn't notice.

'You're just like I was at your age,' she said, laughing and pulling my hair, gently, 'with a bit of Patrick thrown in. You'll be fine.'

I emailed Patrick, saying I had to do a school project on 'What School Was Like in Your Parents' Day.' He wasn't reassuring.

> To: milliethegreatest@mail.com
> From: pmcd@lndonuni.edu.uk
>
> School days. Ha! Don't talk to me
> about SCHOOL. It was simply BARBARIC,
> Millie. It nearly KILLED me.
> I HATED EVERY MINUTE except for
> science and mathematics, which was
> JUST bearable. Even that was RANDOM.
> One year I was stuck with Mr Henshaw
> who knew LESS than I did about
> ALMOST EVERYTHING. Personally, I
> think every child should be tutored
> and schools made OBSOLETE. Better not
> put THAT down, Millie sweet. You
> don't want to put the teachers off.
> But I went to school in the DARK AGES.
>
> LOVE
> patrick.
> ------------------------------------

Of course Patrick had it wrong. It wasn't school I was worried about. That was easy. It was playtime, lunchtime and the camp looming like a hurricane on the horizon. They were the problems. The work was easy.

The library was open during lunchtime and

that's where I went. The lunchtime librarian on Mondays was always Ms O'Brien and she knew everything about fantasy. I asked her to recommend her favourite authors, in alphabetical order. I started reading the A's.

I didn't want to go to school camp because I wouldn't have Mum to come home to in the afternoon or the library at lunchtime. I'd have to spend three hours on a bus and no one would choose me to sit beside. I'd have to share a room with at least seven other girls and they'd all look at me, at my clothes, at my pyjamas, at the stuff I'd brought to do, the CDs I played, the books I read, and they'd know I wasn't one of them. I wasn't sure that I could eat breakfast in front of so many people. I knew they'd be watching me, watching how I ate and checking out my face to see if it looked as bad first thing in the morning as I knew it did. All faces do, but mine in particular does. I've got these little pimples. Mum says not to squeeze them so I don't. Well, I do, because if I don't they look really gross. But they look gross when you do, too. My hair, which is dead straight — that's Patrick's fault — often looks greasy, which isn't fair at all as I wash it every second day. Who could eat their breakfast happily with my face in front of them? And how could I eat my breakfast with all their faces in front of me?

49.

When I get older I'm going to have dreadlocks, wear thick goth make-up and eat breakfast completely by myself.

I made a list of all the things I needed for the camp. These weren't on the official list. These were on my list.

1. **GROOVY** pyjamas. They had to have Felix the cat or butterflies on them. My most loved green frog ones wouldn't do. Not at all.
2. New runners with no holes in them
3. A pair of jeans without holes
4. A good hat
5. Some pimple cover-up
6. A bra. I **HAVE** to have a bra.
7. **DECENT** knickers

I took the list to Mum.

'I don't think it's worth going,' I said. 'Look at what I need and I really do need them, Mum, I'm not kidding. I can't go without this stuff.'

Mum read the list through.

'Seems fair enough to me,' she said. 'I think we can cover all that. Are you sure you need pimple cover-up? I can't actually see any pimples.'

'You're not looking then.'

I couldn't believe she'd just give in like that.

'I look at your face every day, Millie, and I have yet to see any pimple that merits cover-up. But if cover-up is what you need for camp, cover-up you'll have.'

'You're trying to get rid of me, is that it?'

Mum dropped the mug she was drying up.

'I am not,' she said and her face went all pinky.

'Well, why do I have to go then?'

'Because I hope you'll enjoy it, Millie. Because the school has planned this camp so you and all the other kids in your grade get to know each other in a different environment. It's to help you build friendships. You have to go.'

'Is that your last word?'

'Yes,' Mum said firmly, sweeping up the broken pieces of china. 'Yes it is, Millie.'

'You have to drive me to school by 7.30 in the morning.'

'That'll be fine.'

'It's a TAFE morning. You'll be rushed.'

'Millie!'

'Okay, okay.'

I was going to camp even if it killed me.

'It will kill me,' I said.

'School camp never killed anyone,' Mum said, in her I'm-getting-very-cranky voice.

'This might be the first time.'

I left the kitchen then. It was time to get out.

I wondered what the symptoms of bubonic plague were and whether I could fake them. I wondered if Mum would believe me if I had a tummy ache or a headache or suddenly developed an inexplicable limp.

The Felix jammies helped. The boy-leg knickers and matching bra in a Japanese pattern — not sweet little roses but wild pink and red florals on green — helped a little more. Mum forgot the cover-up, on purpose I think, but she got everything else and didn't once wrinkle up her nose at the expense.

While I was packing, she came into my room.

'It's hard fitting in, Millie,' she said. 'I don't think either your dad or I did it particularly well, either.'

She hardly ever called Patrick 'your dad'. He was always Patrick. When he was 'your dad', it was a serious you-are-growing-up-talk. I breathed in deeply.

'I'm okay,' I said.

'I hope you will be, Millie. I hope you find at least one friend. That's all you need, you know, a good friend like Frannie. I really want you to be happy here. I do so want you to be happy, Millie. I finally feel as though I am somewhere I want to be, somewhere I've chosen to be, and things are falling into place for me. I want that to happen for you.'

When Mum said that kind of thing, with that little frowny look, she always made me want to do what she wants.

'I can't promise to love camp,' I said.

'I know that, Millie, but you can promise not to be determined to hate it.'

'Okay,' I said, but I kept the fingers on my right hand crossed. I'd wait to see who I had to sit next to on the bus before I promised that.

CHAPTER SIX

The trip was the worst. I had to sit next to Mr
Lawrence. It wasn't that Mr Lawrence was so bad,
it was more that sitting next to any teacher was
bad, unless it was Ms O'Grady. Everyone adored
Ms O'Grady. She was cool. Kids queued up to sit
next to her. She was pregnant and she let you feel
the baby kick if she liked you. Or that's what
Tayla claimed.

Tayla was the prettiest girl in our grade, if not
the whole school. She had long dark hair that
hung down almost to her bottom. She had perfect
skin and almost-green eyes. She sat some of the
way with Ms O'Grady and then she swapped with
one of her best friends.

Nobody queued up to sit with Mr Lawrence. It was just him and me, all the way to camp. He tried to make conversation, but I didn't feel much like talking, so I did that grunting thing. It put him off after a while and we both pulled books out of our day-packs and read.

The only conversation we managed was just before we pulled in for morning tea, when he happened to catch me trying to glimpse the title of the book he was reading.

'It's just something my wife wants me to read,' he said, a little apologetically, holding up the book.

'*12 Steps to Raising Successful Teens*,' I read. 'My mum's got that, too.'

'Has she? Did she … sorry, Millie. You are clearly a success story. That was rude of me.'

'She hasn't even read it,' I said quickly. 'She doesn't like the person who gave it to her.'

'Ah,' he said. 'Well, I don't think that excuse will work with my wife, unfortunately.'

'You could always drop it in the bath. That worked for me. I always drop books I don't like in the bath. Or I did, when we had a bath. We don't have one in our new house. We've got a shower, of course.'

'I hadn't thought of the bath trick. I have, on occasion, dropped a book in it. Not deliberately, of course. And I've always dried them carefully, in front of the gas heater. Or with my wife's hair dryer. Never totally works. Good idea, Millie. In the bath, eh? Simple but effective. Thank you.'

You can see what I mean when I say no one was queuing up to sit next to Mr Lawrence, although it was quite charming of him to tell me I was a successful teenager, when I so obviously wasn't.

I was in the left-overs dormitory. There's nearly always one of them. Suppose you've got 44 girls from Year Seven. The dorms sleep eight, so you have five rooms of eight and one of four. The girls who don't have special friends are always bunched in the last room.

There weren't even four of us. There was Jess, Daina and myself. Jess was on some kind of medication which made her sleepy and slow. Daina was just a girl who liked to be alone. I guess they might have thought that about me, too, given my lunchtimes in the library. So they put us together, in the left-overs dormitory.

Camp wasn't looking good by anybody's standards.

It got worse. The first day wasn't so bad. We had a choice of activities. They do that on the first day to lull you into the feeling that everything will be all right. After that the pressure was on.

A chart went up in the recreation room. It divided us into four teams. I was in Koala Team.

At least *they* divided us up. There was some complaining about that. Tayla and her gang were split up, as were Helen-Sarah-and-Rachel. Helen and Tayla were in Koala Team. It was clear they hated each other.

Why they think team activities will build trust and friendships is beyond me. In my experience, the person on the team who fumbles the ball, doesn't run fast enough or can't think of a way to get a stupid tyre over a stupid wooden pole is hated, called names and never allowed to forget their failure. So much for trust and friendship!

I knew I would be that person on Koala Team.

I did fumble the ball and I was the only one who had any difficulty scaling the fence in the obstacle course, except for Jess who didn't count because of her medication and Brett who was just plain fat.

But I didn't get called names and my mistakes were hardly noticed. Koala Team was focused on not letting Helen and Tayla kill each other. They picked on each other's tiniest mistakes and hissed and spat at each other like wild cats.

'You dropped that, you've cost us a point,' Tayla said, before Helen had even had a chance to catch, let alone drop, the ball.

Helen retaliated by crossing her arms and not even trying.

'Yeah,' she said, when the ball fell at her feet, 'I sure did. Mind you, if you'd kept your big mouth shut, I might just have been able to catch that.'

'Tayla!' Dion shouted, 'let's just try to finish the course, can we?'

'I'm not interested in playing with a team who doesn't put in one hundred and ten percent.'

'Well, I'm not interested in playing with some stuck-up little nobody who thinks she's the greatest and criticises everyone else as though they're complete losers.'

'Girls, if your whole team isn't playing, you'll be penalised one hundred points, and I mean that!'

'Sorry, Ms O'Grady. See what you've done now?'

'Oh, shut your face, Tayla. Could I care less?'

'It wasn't Helen's fault,' I said, forgetting myself. 'If you'd just stop being so mean, Tayla, we might get somewhere.'

'Oh, what would you know?' Tayla turned the full force of her wrath on to me. 'You aren't even from round here, are you? How come you think you know anything?'

'I know what I saw,' I said, 'and I know what I heard.'

'Oh, do you? Well, I know what I saw on the obstacle course and that was you going around that fence without even trying.'

'I did try. I'm just not good at things like that.'

'Not good at much, are you, Millie Mouse? You cheated. You could get us disqualified for that.'

'Tayla Cameron, what is going on here?'

'Nothing Ms O'Grady. We're just discussing our group and negotiating role changes, that's all.'

'It sounds more like shouting,' Ms O'Grady said. 'Helen, come here. I want to talk to you. Team, take 50 points off for not finishing and a further 25 off for disputes. Then go and have some afternoon tea.'

'See what you've done, Millie Mouse the big cheat, you've upset Ms O'Grady. You shouldn't upset pregnant women. You might make something happen to the baby.'

'That's just rubbish,' I said. 'Honestly, Tayla, how do you expect to get away with that kind of stuff? She's not upset, anyway. She's just doing her job.'

'What would you know about Ms O'Grady? Do you know that she lost a baby last year? Well, do you?'

'No. No, I didn't know that.'

'It's true. The baby was born early. Stress, my mother said. She'd know. She's a nurse. Bet you didn't know that, Millie Mouse.'

I watched Ms O'Grady walking away with Helen. She was looking serious and shaking her head, but I didn't think we had stressed her.

'I'm not doing any more of this,' Tayla said. 'I feel sick. I've got a headache right here.' She pressed her temples with her pink sparkly fingernails.

'Yeah, right.'

'Millie, where do you get off being such a b-word. I get headaches. I get migraines. Sometimes I have to stay in bed for two days. The pain is so great that I faint if I have to get up. That's what I think I'm getting now. You don't care about anyone other than yourself, do you? You don't care if Ms O'Grady loses another baby. You don't care if I get a migraine. You're just so selfish.'

I watched her saunter off. I couldn't believe what she had just said. I did care about people. I turned to Dion, but she was busy tying up her shoelaces.

'I care about people,' I said to her anyway. 'I didn't know about Ms O'Grady. How was I to know?'

'Everybody knows about Ms O'Grady,' Dion said in a flat voice, 'and everyone knows Tayla gets bad migraines. She fainted during a tennis match once. She'd gone on with a migraine so she didn't let her doubles partner down. She's a state champion.'

'How does everyone know?'

'Everyone knows about Ms O'Grady because it

happened last year when Tayla's brother was in her class. And everyone knows about Tayla because she was the under-12 champion for two years in a row. Everyone in Stockie Primary knew that.'

'Well, I didn't go to Stockie.'

'Tayla's right. You don't know much.'

We had fruit and biscuits for afternoon tea. You were allowed one piece of fruit and two biscuits. Then it was free time. Some kids played table tennis in the recreation room. Others went for walks, kicked a soccer ball around or practised netball. I went to the dorm, lay down on my bed and read for a while.

Helen interrupted me.

'Ms O'Grady wants to see you,' she said, poking her head in without even knocking. 'She's in the dining room.'

I clutched the book to my chest. Why would she want to see me?

As if reading my mind, Helen said, 'I bet Tayla's been telling her stuff. But don't worry, Millie, I'll be a witness if you need one. Ms O'Grady's cool. She listens. You're probably just going to get the poor Tayla talk.'

'The what?'

'You'll see.' And with that Helen disappeared.

I walked as slowly as I could over to the dining

room. Kookaburras nearby laughed at me. Normally I love kookaburras. They are one of my favourite birds. I love the shape of them and the flash of blue in their wings and I love their laughter. It sounds as though they are inviting the world to share their wonderful, wild joke. But this afternoon it sounded as though I was the joke.

Ms O'Grady was sitting at the edge of one of the tables, a cup of tea in front of her.

'Sit down, Millie,' she said, indicating a chair that was pulled out a little, so I would be facing her. 'Do you want a drink of something? I could rustle you up a tea, if you drink it?'

'No, thank you,' I said. 'I had some cordial with my fruit.'

'How are you getting on, Millie, at school? Are you enjoying it?'

'It's okay.'

'You've come from a different town, haven't you?'

'Yes.' Why everyone thought if you didn't live in this town you were an alien was beyond me.

'That's hard, isn't it? I remember when I first came here. I knew everyone thought I was some kind of weird hippy chick from the big city. I didn't think I'd ever fit in. I cried practically every night for about a month. My husband thought I'd gone mad. Then things changed. I got to know people.

People got to know me. I made friends. I realised that some of the people I thought were cold-shouldering me felt a little threatened by my city background.'

'I don't come from the city,' I said. 'Mum and I lived in the country. A little country town.'

'I realise that,' Ms O'Grady said, 'but you are a bit exotic, Millie.'

'I don't know what you mean.'

'I think if you go home and think about it, you might.' Ms O'Grady smiled at me. I had to drop my eyes. Hers were too kind and I thought I'd burst into tears. I looked at her stomach instead, round as a shell under her stretchy skirt. Just as I looked, her whole tummy kind of rippled.

'Oh!' She laughed. 'This baby's going to be a dancer. Feel that, Millie!' And she grabbed my hand and placed it on her stomach.

It was amazing. You could actually feel life in there. It was bizarre, kind of scary and kind of wonderful at the same time. I couldn't imagine what it felt like for her.

'Are you scared?' I blurted out, unable to stop myself.

'Yes, I am a bit,' Ms O'Grady said, 'but then I look around at all you kids and I think, well, Theresa, they've all been born and their mums and dads coped. That makes me feel a little bit better. Your mum was fine, wasn't she? And your dad?'

'Patrick loves me,' I said, 'but he doesn't live with us. He's a scientist and has to be overseas. Mum did most of the coping by herself. But, yeah, I guess she was fine. I guess you have to be when you have a baby to look after, don't you? I mean, it isn't just you anymore, is it?'

'Most people think like you do, Millie. But some people don't handle it as well as others. Tayla's mum, for example, didn't handle anything well. She had a breakdown after Tayla was born and couldn't look after her. That's been hard for Tayla and her dad. Tayla's done very well to get to where she is now, believe me. I know she can be … a little domineering, but when she is like that, remember that she doesn't have a mum around like you have. Okay?'

I shrugged. I wanted to say, I don't have a dad around and Sheri doesn't live with us anymore so what are you going to do about that? But I didn't, because my hand was still tingling from feeling Ms O'Grady's baby and I didn't want to upset her in case anything happened to it.

'I know things haven't necessarily been easy for you, either. But Millie, I look at you and I see a strong person with their own wonderful destiny to follow. You're an individual. You'll be fine. Tayla's

64.

different. She's dependent on that little group she's got. She's nothing without them. Do you understand?'

'You have to have friends,' I said.

'Friends are good, but for some people hangers-on are essential. You'll make friends, Millie. Just give yourself a bit of time. Now, hop out and get some fresh air.'

I stood up to go.

'By the way, Millie,' she said, 'be brave about the rumours, too. Tayla's saying you don't care about anyone and that you wanted to give her a migraine. No one will believe her. We all know better. But keep your chin up, okay?'

'Thanks,' I muttered. I couldn't look at her.

Minutes after I got back to my dormitory, Helen arrived, almost as though she had been watching for me.

'Wasn't too bad?' she asked, plonking herself down on my bed uninvited.

'No.' I surreptitiously wiped my eyes.

'See, told you.'

'Ms O'Grady said Tayla's been saying I wanted to give her a migraine.'

'Who cares? She's toe-jam. Sarah and Rachel and I wanted to know if you'd like to be in our Red Faces team. Of course, since we've been practising for weeks at school, you'll only be a dancer and you'll have to learn quickly, but it doesn't matter if you make mistakes. We all do.'

I'd forgotten about the Red Faces competition. Forgotten or managed to ignore it. This was the other camp torture. We all had to make up an act and perform it in front of everyone. I had nothing planned.

'I'm not very good at dancing,' I said.

'Neither are we. So that's a yes?'

'Yes.'

'Good, I'll go and get the others and then we can work out a costume for you.'

'Okay.'

She dashed out the door. Helen didn't seem to do anything slowly. A costume! I wondered what they'd have thought up. I felt suddenly excited about everything, even the idea of dancing, although it was a panicky excitement. What happened if I did it wrong? But I was okay at dancing. Sheri, Mum and I had often danced around the lounge room and Sheri said I had natural rhythm. I did a few practise steps and watched in the mirror.

I was not exactly tall for my age, but I wasn't hopelessly short, either. My hair was dead straight but at least it was thick and Mum had let me grow it past my shoulders as soon as I'd stopped going to Newland Primary School. I'd had it shorter there because of the head lice. We bred superior nits at Newland. I think they'd mutated.

My eyes were brown with gold speckles. My face was too long, my chin was too stubborn and my mouth was on the small size. It wasn't the face of a movie star, although it might have done for a minor role in one of those movies nobody much sees. Or an extra in something. It would be cool to be a movie extra. They get to mutter *rhubarb, rhubarb, rhubarb* in crowd scenes and get really close to a lot of famous people.

I was daydreaming about being an extra on a set with Orlando Bloom – how I'd pick up something he didn't know he'd dropped. A love letter, or something really precious. I'd run after him and say, 'Excuse me, sir, you dropped this', and hold it out to him with shaking fingers.

'Don't be nervous, my pretty one,' he'd say (ignoring my stubborn chin and my little mouth), 'and thank you a thousand times. This means more to me than my whole fee for this movie. I owe you. I owe you dinner at the restaurant of your choice, whatever you'd like to eat, wherever in the entire world and whenever. You name the date, the place, and I will be there.'

Helen opened the door and walked in, followed by Sarah and Rachel.

'Do you have anything we can turn into a belly-dancing costume?' she asked. 'We found a spare

67.

scarf for you.'

I left Orlando gazing adoringly after me while I returned to reality.

'Belly dancing!' I squeaked. 'Oh, I don't think I can do that in front of people. Not belly dancing!'

CHAPTER SEVEN

We didn't get First Prize, which was a packet of lollypops. But fortunately we didn't get Funniest Act either, which was a possibility since Sarah's scarf came undone and I tripped over it, bumped into Helen and sent us both crashing down to the floor.

Tayla and her gang started slow clapping at that point, but Ms O'Grady quelled them with a glance. Tayla's migraine seemed to have disappeared just in time for her to do a lip-synched number to some song about boys and love.

Okay, our song was about boys and love as well. That's just what songs are about. But we didn't shake our bottoms the way she did and we didn't strut around either. We shimmied a bit, or we tried to — that's when Sarah's scarf came undone. But we weren't rude. Tayla didn't get First Prize, either. But then, nor did anyone actually laugh at her.

I didn't care. I'd survived Red Faces and I had made friends, at least for the time being.

'Oh well,' Helen said, as we drank hot chocolate with marshmallows later, 'there's always next year.'

'I think that scarf was too slippery,' Sarah said, 'but at least we were dressed. Not like Tayla, wearing her PJs.'

'She had to wear them,' Rachel said, 'for the song. I can understand that. It wouldn't have made sense of that line, "and I'm dreaming of you, dreaming of you, as I tuck myself into my little bed, I'm dreaming of you, dreaming of you in my head".'

'That line sucks,' Helen said. 'The whole song sucks.'

'She didn't win, anyway,' Rachel said. 'But fancy that stupid Aidan's joke winning. It wasn't even funny. I didn't get it, did you?'

'Not really. I got lost in the middle somewhere. But I think he did, too. I think they gave it to Aidan because he never wins anything.'

'I think they gave it to him because he put on funny voices and did that little bow at the end,' I said. I had enjoyed Aidan's joke. I did get it — it was about an IT person and a talking frog he doesn't kiss because he wants to have a talking frog in his pocket rather than a beautiful girl because IT people don't have time for a social life. It was one of those goes-on-forever jokes. Patrick had sent it to me in an email — that's how come I got it.

'Yes, I think you're right. That's called performance,' Sarah said, 'and they're keen on performance. They think if you can perform, you must have high self-esteem.'

'I don't get this self-esteem stuff,' Rachel said. 'Why do we all have to have it?'

'It's when you feel good about yourself,' Helen said. 'Come on, Rachel, you know that.'

'But I don't think you can feel good about yourself all the time,' Rachel objected. 'I mean, what about on days when your favourite jeans don't do up, or you step in dog poo, or your mum shouts at you because she's had a fight with her boyfriend? You don't feel good about yourself then, do you?'

'Well, you should. It's more than what just goes on, it's something else. Oh, Rachel, I can't explain it. You'll have to ask Ms O'Grady.'

'It's about feeling good about yourself deep

down,' I said, 'so that those things don't affect what's in your heart. They stay surface things that you get over without falling apart, because you're strong about who you really are.'

'Wow, that's right!' Helen said. 'Do you get it now, Rachel?'

'Yeah, but I don't know that I've got it.'

'We're learning to get it this year,' Sarah said. 'They'll teach you, Rache, and then you'll be fine.'

'So it's like Maths? You reckon you learn it?' I felt unsure. It didn't seem entirely right to me.

'You can learn everything,' Helen said.

'You can't learn everything.'

'Well, come on, Rachel, you tell me one thing you can't learn.'

There was silence while we all thought. Finally Rachel said, 'You can't learn how to do sex.'

Sarah and I put our fingers in our mouths and made gagging noises, but Helen said, 'Well, I reckon you probably can. It's just like Maths, Rachel — you don't want to learn it but they make you. Sex is just the same.'

Mr Lawrence and Shirley, Caitlin's mum, came over, and we stopped talking about sex and self-esteem and talked about reality TV instead. It was safer.

The next day it poured rain. It wasn't just spit spot drizzle that they can still send you out in —

appropriately dressed, of course. This was bucketing down, just like it had when Mum had her interview. You could see the despair on the teachers' faces. What were they going to do with us all?

'I knew it would rain,' Helen said, watching it from the recreation room window. She drew little love hearts on the window. 'It always does when you go away anywhere. It's one of those rules.'

'Barbeque — rain,' I said.

'Wash the car — rain,' Rachel said.

'Plan a picnic — rain,' Mr Lawrence said, coming up behind us. 'So we thought we might have a games morning. Did anyone bring any games?'

'I brought a chess set,' I said very quietly. It was a nerdy thing to do and I couldn't even play properly yet.

'Ah, well done, Millie.' Mr Lawrence beamed. 'So we've got two chess sets, two scrabble boards, three games of monopoly, table tennis, UNO cards, playing cards and one game of Trivial Pursuit. That's the ticket. We'll all be nicely occupied.'

Mr Lawrence was either stupid or very optimistic.

'Boring,' everyone chorused when he read out the list, and people wandered off wired up to music or Game Boys.

I didn't have a CD player or a Game Boy. I did have a book, though, and I read in one of the fluffy bean bags until the Lady's unicorn was speared to death and then I couldn't read anymore, just for a little while. I looked around the room. Most of the kids had gone off to lie on their beds in the dorms and complain about the weather.

Mr Lawrence was reading at a table. He sighed as he read and I guessed what he was reading. I felt sorry for him and went over to him.

'Ah, Millie.' He looked up quickly and smiled at me as though I'd rescued him. 'How is your book then?'

'They've killed our Lady's unicorn,' I said, 'so it's got pretty sad. There was a prophecy about it, too. That when it died terror on the land would be unleashed and "violence and sadness unceasing would cause the tears to join like oceans". The hunters were warned to take the prophecy seriously. Of course they didn't. The unicorn was too fine a prize, silver horn and silver hoofs. It's just greed, Mr Lawrence.'

'Well, yes, you're right about that, Millie. Greed rules the world.' He closed the book and rubbed the children's faces on the cover absently as though he was cleaning them. 'You enjoy reading fantasy? Have you read Ursula le Guin yet?'

I shook my head.

'What a treat you have ahead of you! Start with *A Wizard of Earthsea*, and the others in the series, of course. A marvellous mind, that woman, just marvellous. When you've done with those, read *The Left Hand of Darkness*. Though you might wait a bit for that one.'

'Thanks, I'll write them down in my journal. I've got a list of books I need to read. How's your book going?'

'Confidentially, Millie, it strikes me that I might fail Parenting, really. The book says "make time to talk to your kids", but when I ask my kids what's going on, they always say "nothing". It doesn't make for a deep conversation. And my boy doesn't even say that. He just grunts.'

'Maybe you aren't asking the right questions,' I said. Mr Lawrence's face was all droop. His mouth drooped at the corners, his eyes drooped at their corners and even his forehead wrinkles seemed to be heading down towards his chin. It made him look sad – except for when he smiled, when all the lines headed right up in the other direction.

'No, I'm probably not asking the right questions,' he admitted, 'but it's hard to know what the right questions are. That's what I find. "How are things going?" "Yep." "Do you need anything?" "Yep." That's always money, of course. They do seem to need an awful lot of money. Their mother has better luck with them.'

'You could try taking them to dinner,' I said, suddenly inspired. 'That's what my mother and I do sometimes, when we feel a bit depressed. Then you have to talk to each other because you shouldn't read in a café, right? And there's no television. So there's nothing to do but talk. To start off, you might just talk about the food. But pretty soon you're talking, you know, really talking.'

'That's an excellent idea, Millie. I think I'll try that.'

'The other thing you could do, Mr Lawrence, if you don't mind me suggesting it ...'

'Not at all. Suggest away!'

'Well, people lose things at camp all the time. So instead of the bath idea, you could do the camp thing and lose your book here. I bet she wouldn't bother buying you a new one, not if the dinner thing works. She won't need to, will she?'

'That's the ticket, Millie, that's a great idea. Under the bed, I think, don't you?'

'Under the mattress might be safer,' I said. 'Under our beds are pretty clean. Rachel checked because of her asthma. The cleaners do a good job. But under the mattress was pretty grotty.'

'Thanks. Now is there anything I can do for you?'

'Well, I was wondering if you play chess. See, I

don't really know how to play but Patrick, my dad, does and I want to be able to impress him when he's next in Australia. It's good to throw something new at him, Mum says. It keeps him on his toes.'

Mr Lawrence and I played chess until it was time for dinner. I liked Mr Lawrence. There was something Patrick-y about him, even though he wasn't a drama queen. He felt safe. I was sorry he was married. If Mum was man-hunting again I wouldn't be so worried if she turned up with someone like Mr Lawrence. Even though he was years older than Mum, and obviously thought brown was a power colour, judging from his taste in jumpers.

Camp wasn't as bad as it could have been and the trip home was great. Helen-Sarah-and-Rachel and I sat together, not in the back row, because Tayla and her gang had baggsed that, but we sat behind each other and talked.

'Mum will be pleased I'm home,' Helen said. 'She worries when I'm at camp. She gets lonely.'

'Yeah, my mum will be pleased, too,' I said. '*I* worry about *her* when I'm at camp.'

'Mum'll be pleased to see me,' Rachel said, 'but Terry won't.'

'Who's Terry?'

'Mum's boyfriend. They've been going out for

nearly three months and when he heard about the camp he booked them into a motel for two nights, like they were on their honeymoon or something.'

Sarah and Helen made throwing-up noises.

'No, it's cool,' Rachel said. 'He's okay, really. First thing he did, he gave me a TV. Honest. So I could watch it in my room while they cuddled on the couch. But that's cool. I get to watch whatever I like, and if I turn it right down I can watch when they've gone to bed. What about your mum, Millie? Does she have a boyfriend?'

'No,' I said, 'she has Patrick. Well, she doesn't exactly. They're just friends.'

'Are you sure? That's what they say, you know, before it happens.'

'Patrick's my father,' I said, 'so it's already happened, and they're friends now. He's overseas anyway. He's a scientist.'

'So she hasn't met anyone else?'

'No.'

'Wait until she does. You'll have to worry more about her then!'

'Why?'

'Oh, you know, they forget things sometimes. Mind you, it can be good. Sometimes they forget to make you do your homework.'

I wondered about Mum. She hadn't even asked me about homework lately. And she'd broken something, too, when I'd told her it felt as though she wanted to get rid of me.

'Do they break things?' I asked. 'You know, just drop them out of the blue?'

'I don't think Mum's ever broken anything,' Rachel said, 'but she rear-ended a parked car. I don't think that was love though. It was more like new contact lenses. She got the contacts just after she met Terry — she thought glasses made her look older. So you could say love caused it, in a roundabout way.'

'I'm never going to fall in love,' Helen said. 'Never in a million years. It makes you do stupid things. My mum started singing. You know, really singing, while she did anything. It was embarrassing. And they'd have these really long phone calls.'

Mum sang. But she'd always been a shower and morning singer. That's why we had the CD player in the kitchen.

'That's because they're happy,' Sarah said. 'I think it's beautiful.'

'But you can say that, Sarah, because your mum and dad are still married. You'd be saying something different if they got divorced and your mum got a boyfriend.'

'So when you say happy,' I interrupted, 'do you mean just happy, or happy happy?'

'Happy happy,' Helen said immediately. 'You know, take-aways because who can be bothered, singing, new clothes, smiling the secret smile all the time.'

Had Mum been happy happy, or just happy?

When Mum met me at the bus she didn't look any different. She just looked like the same old Kate. She even had her painting gear on. That didn't seem to indicate boyfriend evidence. She looked, well, messy and paint-dabbed.

'How was camp, sweetheart?'

'It was great,' I said. 'And I'd like you to meet my new friends. This is Helen-Sarah-and-Rachel, my mother, Kate.'

'Well, girls, I am pleased to meet you!' Mum said. 'You'll all have to come over soon for afternoon tea.'

'That would be cool, Mrs ... I mean, Kate,' the girls chorused in their Helen-Sarah-and-Rachel voice, and I knew that camp had been truly great.

CHAPTER EIGHT

In the middle of the best week of school ever, Helen invited me to her house for a sleep-over. We were practising netball. Sarah and Rachel were sitting on the grass talking about boys.

'Saturday night?' I repeated, fumbling a defence I should have got. 'Saturday night? I'll have to ask Mum.'

'My mum works at the TAFE, too,' Helen said. 'She said she'd look out for your mum in the staff room and introduce herself. She works in Access.'

'I don't think Mum goes to the staff room.' I wasn't sure but it didn't feel like the kind of thing Mum would do.

'Everyone goes to the staff room,' Helen said.

'That's where the coffee is. You know what they're like about coffee.'

Sure enough, when Mum got home from work that afternoon, she said, 'I met the mother of one of your new friends, Millie. And she says her daughter has asked you to sleep-over. Is that great or what? You've got a better social life than me!'

'I won't go if you're going to be lonely,' I said. 'It's okay, honest. I can see them at school.'

'Don't be silly,' Mum said. 'Of course you'll go. You want to go, don't you?'

'Yes, yes I do. But I don't …'

'I'll be fine,' Mum said. 'We're finalising things for this exhibition anyway, the one I inherited? I told you about it.'

'Oh, sure.' I couldn't really remember but that was okay. If Mum had work to do, she'd be fine without me.

'And then,' she continued, 'I might go to the movies.'

'By yourself?'

'Depends.' She shrugged, turning away. 'Someone from the exhibition committee might be interested. There's a good film on at the Valley cinema.'

'So you really don't mind?'

'Of course not. I think this is a great

opportunity, Millie. Helen's mother seems very nice. It was funny really, because we had coffee together only last week but didn't put two and two together. About you girls, I mean.'

'I wasn't friends with Helen-Sarah-and-Rachel last week,' I pointed out.

'That's true,' Mum said. 'Things can happen fast, can't they?'

'That was the whole point of the camp, to bond us together. You said so yourself.'

'That's right, I did. Now, Millie, what shall we have for dinner?'

After dinner the phone rang. I don't mean that was unusual. Sheri often rang us, Patrick rang at least once a week, and there were other friends from our old life, too. What was unusual was that when the phone rang, Mum took the call and then sent me off to the shower and took the phone into her bedroom.

She was off the phone by the time I got out, and was drinking a cup of tea.

'Who was that?' I asked casually.

'Just someone from the exhibition committee,' Mum said.

'What is this exhibition anyway?' I asked.

'An exhibition for the Diploma students,' Mum said. 'It was supposed to be on late last year, but the tutor was ill. So we're doing it this year, instead. I thought I told you all this. It's occupied most of my non-teaching time for the past six weeks!'

'Just refreshing my memory,' I said smoothly. 'Any chocolate biscuits left?'

The phone rang again much later. I was in bed reading. I waited for Mum to come in and tell me who had rung up but she was on the phone for so long I went to sleep waiting. She was on for so long it could only have been one person in the world — and that was Sheri.

Helen-Sarah-and-Rachel-and-I played netball practically every fine day. We weren't on a team or anything. It was just what we did. We weren't on a team because:

- Helen didn't like competitive sports.
- Sarah was too short.
- Rachel played badminton and she was only allowed to play one thing after school.
- I didn't really play netball at all.

'You should though,' Helen said, 'you've got the height, Millie, and you're fast, when you think about it.'

I didn't like having to think fast, although I loved the feeling when the ball soared out of your hands and went up, up into the air and then straight into the basket, as though it was destined to drop through from the moment it left your hands, tugged there by an invisible thread. The rules confused me, though, and I didn't like the way everyone shouted at you, 'Throw it here, here, here!' I agreed with Helen about competitive sports, although it wasn't so much the competition as the noise and the pressure.

I liked hanging out with Helen-Sarah-and-Rachel. They talked to each other about everything, even the embarrassing stuff.

'I like Drew because he's funny,' Rachel said, lying back in the grass. 'Do you see that big cloud, the one over there. I reckon it looks like a dragon.'

'Like the dragon from *The Dragon Piper*,' Sarah said. 'That has to be the best book ever written.'

'I haven't read it.'

'Oh, Millie, it is so good. You'll just love it.'

'You will love it, Millie. Sarah, can you lend it to Millie?'

'Of course, I'll bring it to school tomorrow. I know what you mean about Drew, Rachel, he is funny. But he's too short for you, really.'

'I don't care if he's short,' Rachel said. 'I don't get all that stuff about boys having to be taller. Anyway, if I have to find a taller boy I'm going to be in trouble. That's what my dad says. He says I should get used to looking down on boys. He says that's the natural order of things anyway.'

'You'll just have to wear flat shoes,' Helen said.

'You can wear whatever shoes you want,' Sarah said, 'and if he really likes you, he won't care.'

'I think boys are overrated,' Helen said, 'and we talk about them way too much.'

We got the first term project that day. It was the big one:

'My Environment — What I Love, What I Hate.'

'A chance for everyone to get down and personal,' Ms O'Grady said, smiling around the class as though she hadn't announced the worse news in the world. 'I expect to see some really fantastic individual takes on this subject. I expect you all to do some research, but that research can be quite original. You can interview people, go online, look up current environmental news items — anything you have to do to make the project your own. I certainly don't want to see a lot of half-baked, rushed projects with no thought put into them. I know we have some excellent scholars in this class and I expect to see the evidence!'

'I hate projects,' Rachel said, dragging her bag along the footpath after school.

'My mum hates projects,' Helen said. 'She said they should be banned. They're simply too much work for the parents.'

'I don't mind them,' I said cautiously, 'but I

don't think I've lived in this town long enough to know anything about it, so this project is going to be really hard.'

'I wonder if I could just do it on my room,' Sarah said. 'I mean, that's my real environment, isn't it? I wonder if Ms O'Grady would let me do that?'

'It can't just be your room,' Rachel said. 'It's an environmental project, not a room project.'

'Yeah, well, my room is an environment,' Sarah said. 'I mean, it's got its own living systems happening in it. Or that's what mum says, anyway. Under the bed, you know, and the apple core in my bedside table drawer — the one that went mouldy.'

I shelved the project for the time being as too hard. I had other problems to deal with, problems I didn't really want to talk about with Helen-Sarah-and-Rachel. Not yet.

First, there was the sleep-over and that was okay. I was looking forward to that. I panicked a bit about what I'd take, but I talked it over with Helen and found out that I'd need:

1. A pair of muck-around jeans.
2. One good, going-to-the-movies outfit.
3. A book for reading in bed on Sunday morning.
4. A teddy if I wanted one - Helen couldn't

sleep without hers.
5. My journal, of course.
6. My mum's phone number in case anything
went wrong.

My real problem was a boy at school. I could hardly even say his name, not without feeling myself go red. I couldn't write it in my journal, not properly. I called him by his initials and then disguised them by doing them in fake Elizabethan writing with lots of curls and loops:

R. H.

He had this curly mouth, curly hair and crinkly eyes, and he smiled so much that everyone called him Smiley. He was good at everything. Well, not everything. He was lousy at Maths and Italian, and he couldn't sing to save his life. But he was great at soccer, basketball and football. I liked him because he smiled all the time and he was one of the popular kids who didn't seem to care that he was popular.

I had a crush on him. I knew it was a crush because I could tick off every single crush indicator on the list Helen had compiled. Helen knew all about crushes. She had her first crush when she was in Preps, she said.

Helen's Seven-Point Crush Indicator List

1. You look at the boy all the time.
2. You tease him a lot.
3. When other people tease him you
        defend him.
4. You blush when people use your name and
        his name in the same sentence.
5. You worry about your clothes and
        hair more.
6. You try to get interested in the stuff
        he's interested in.
7. If he's popular, you act stuck-up.

I did everything, even the last thing. I did act kind of stuck-up around him. Not mega stuck-up, not I'm-too-posh-for-you-to-clean-my-shoes stuck up, just I've-got-better-things-to-talk-about-than-your-game-of-soccer-but-if-you-ask-me-twice-I'll-answer kind of stuck-up.

I had a crush on *R.H.* and I felt like all the things that were on Helen's 'How You Feel When You've Got a Mega Crush Six-Point Indicator List':

1. Airy fairy
2. Bad, really bad
3. Good, really good - particularly when he
        looks at you

4. Scared - that he doesn't like you
5. Scared - that he likes someone else
6. Scared - that he likes you

I had my first crush and I had it badly. Maybe it was like those diseases that if you don't get them when you're a kid you get them three times as badly when you're an adult. I was a late developer when it came to crushes and it was like killer chicken pox.

CHAPTER NINE

When I got home from the sleep-over, Mum seemed weird. Usually if I've been away she's all questions, questions, questions. This time she opened the front door and looked almost surprised it was me.

'Oh, hi Millie,' she said, 'you're home early.'

'No, I'm not,' I said, dropping my bag so I could hug her. 'It's about five past six, actually.'

'Of course, so it is.' She hugged me quickly. 'Have a good time?'

'It was brilliant. Really great. We stayed up until late last night, watching videos and talking. Helen's mother's cool, too. She's a low-maintenance mother. You know, here's the popcorn, girls, don't burn it.

And Helen's bedroom is fantastic. She's got all these posters everywhere — not just movie star posters, although she's got some of those, but animals, too. It's great.'

'Good. I'm pleased you had such a good time,' Mum said. 'I think we'll have noodles for dinner, take-away noodles. Is that okay?'

I followed her into the kitchen.

'I haven't quite finished cleaning up in here,' she said. 'Millie, why don't you unpack your bag and sort out your washing.' And she almost shooed me out of the kitchen, but not before I'd noticed the mess.

'What were you doing?' I asked, peering over her shoulder. There was a pile of stuff on the sink — saucepans, wine glasses, plates. 'Mum, it looks as though you've had a party!'

'No party,' she said, trying to block my view. 'Not a party, really. Just dinner, that's all. Come on, Millie, I need that washing.' Mum looked flustered and quite pink.

'How many people came over?'

'Oh, you know, just a couple of people from the exhibition committee. That's all. It was pretty impromptu, really.'

'What does that mean?'

'When something happens on the spur of the moment. Come on, Millie, washing!'

'I need a drink first,' I said and pushed past her into the kitchen.

On the kitchen sink there were:

- Mum's good heavy casserole dish from France
- two wine glasses
- two of the best plates
- two of the lettuce-leaf plates Sheri gave us one Christmas
- two coffee mugs
- two tea cups, the cobalt blue ones Patrick gave us one Christmas
- two bowls with leftover porridge sticking to the sides
- two ordinary glasses
- one porridge saucepan
- one bowl with leftover salad sticking to the sides
- one milk jug
- the orange juicer

'How many people?' I asked pointedly.

'One,' Mum said, sighing, 'just one.'

'And they stayed over?'

'Would you rather someone stay over or drink and drive, Millie?'

'Well, stay over, of course,' I said. 'Did you

change my sheets?'

'Your sheets? No, of course not.'

'Well, I don't want to sleep in used sheets,' I said.

'Oh, okay. Well, you change them then,' Mum said. 'Put them in the wash with your other washing. Now, can you get out of my hair. I have to get rid of this mess.'

'Did you have a nice dinner?' I asked. Mum looked stressed and tired and I thought she needed cheering up.

'Yes, I did. Thanks, Millie. It was a lovely evening.' She turned away from the sink and hugged me. 'And I'm really pleased you had a good time, too.'

When I went to get my sheets I was pretty surprised. The bed was exactly as I had left it. Nothing looked disturbed at all. Whoever had spent last night in my bed had even replaced Merlin exactly where I had left him, half tucked under the doona.

As soon as I had sorted out my washing, I took the phone into my room and rang Helen.

'It looks bad,' she said, 'but it might just *look* bad. Phone Rachel and see what she thinks.'

'Definitely a boyfriend,' Rachel said, as I outlined the kitchen sink contents. 'Two of everything has to be boyfriend.'

'What will I do?' I wailed.

'Well, you can either ask her straight out or wait,' Rachel said. 'It depends.'

'On what?'

'Boyfriends make mums feel guilty,' Rachel said, 'so if you want some new jeans or a new book or a CD now is the time to strike.'

'Don't you think that's mean?'

'It's life,' Rachel said.

'I'll have to think about that,' I said and hung up. I rang Sarah. She actually had two parents who still lived together. She was an endangered species, but it meant that she'd be able to look at the morals of it all objectively.

'You don't even know if it is a boyfriend,' Sarah said, 'although the evidence does suggest it. Maybe she wanted you to find out, do you reckon? Like what Ms O'Grady was saying about that book, you know, where the girl left all the stuff lying around so her mum would find out that she was on drugs? It's a cry for help.'

'It can't be a cry for help if it's a boyfriend.'

'He mightn't even be a boyfriend yet,' Sarah said.

'There were porridge bowls,' I pointed out.

'Oh, he's a boyfriend then. And she wanted you to find out otherwise she'd have done the washing-up right away. I bet she tells you over take-aways.

That's why they get take-aways — it's to make you feel good about what they're going to tell you.'

'So I shouldn't ask her?'

'I'd wait,' Sarah said. 'I think she'd feel better.'

Helen agreed.

'She'll feel in control then,' Helen said. 'They like that. Then you want to meet him as quickly as possible and check him out. Boyfriends can be really cool, but only if they want you to like them. If he doesn't want you to like him, get rid of him.'

'What?'

'You'll have to,' Helen said. 'Mum had one like that. I had to get rid of him. You only want the best ones to stick around. The others will end up being creepy anyway and hurting your mum. You don't want that to happen. So you have to meet him and test him.'

'Millie! Are you on the phone?'

'I've got to go,' I said. 'I'll talk to you tomorrow.'

I hadn't thought of creepy boyfriends, but what if Mum was with someone like old Pig's Trotters? That would be the worst thing in the world. I couldn't let that happen to her. I'd have to save her.

I waited until we'd bought take-away noodles. I waited right through the noodles. Mum cleared her throat a couple of times but nothing happened. She said it was the satay sauce, and it might have been, but it might also have been the word 'boyfriend' sticking there like a fish bone.

I waited right through the 'Worlds Forgotten by Time'. We watched in silence as various archaeologists talked excitedly about chipped pots. 'Worlds' finished and before we could sit through another program in total silence, the phone rang and Mum dived to get it.

'I'll get it,' she practically screamed at me.

'I've got it,' I said, holding it aloft. 'Hello, Millie Childes speaking. Yes, she is. May I say who's calling? It's for you,' I said. 'Someone called Tom Grafton. On the exhibition committee, I suppose.'

I said the last bit in my most sarcastic voice, but Mum didn't seem to notice. She was too busy grabbing the phone and leaving the room with it. What did people do before portable handsets?

The call took ages. When she finally came out, I said, in my meanest voice, 'So I suppose that's the exhibition committee who came to dinner and stayed for breakfast? Also known as *The Boyfriend*?'

'Oh, Millie,' Mum said and hugged me. Her face was flushed and her eyes were all soft and gooey. She looked the way I felt when I looked at *R.H.*

I felt sorry for her and hugged her back.

'Why didn't you tell me?' I asked. 'You've always told me things before.'

'I was waiting to see if it was … you know,

serious or not.'

'So is it? Is he a "boyfriend"?'

'I guess he is. It's pretty weird having a boyfriend at my age, but "man friend" sounds ...'

'Weirder,' I said. 'Is he nice? Will I like him? Will he like me? When do I get to meet him?'

'Steady on. Yes, he is nice. I think you'll like him. I think he'll like you. You'll get to meet each other at the exhibition opening which is on Friday night. Okay? He wants to meet you too, Millie.'

'What does he do?'

'Well, he is kind of on the exhibition committee. He's in the photography department.'

'So he's an artist, too? I don't think artists should live together, Mum.'

'We're not even talking about living together, Millie!' Mum said. 'And he started photography as a technical photographer but, yes, I think he is an artist.'

'That's okay, I quite like artists. Although they don't earn much money and it's not good for there to be two in the one house.'

I could see why Mum was nervous on Friday. When I got home from school she was in the bathroom, getting ready. We had two and a half hours before zero hour, but she was shut in there already.

'Scrubbing off paint,' she called out.

When I put my head around the door to ask what there was to eat, she was wearing a face mask. It was blue. She looked like an alien.

'Is that for *The Boyfriend's* benefit?' I asked. I had counted the phone calls — he had rung her three times that week. They both worked at the same place, for heaven's sake.

'Why doesn't he just come round?' I'd asked after the second phone call. 'It would be cheaper.'

'We're both busy,' Mum had said.

'Not too busy to spend an hour on the phone,' I'd pointed out. I was becoming more of a scientist every day.

'No, it's not just for Tom's benefit,' Mum said. 'Okay, I guess I do want to look my best, but not just for Tom. It's the exhibition and the students. This is my first kind of public thing in the department. I'm feeling anxious.'

I made her a cup of tea without her even asking.

'Millie, what are you going to wear?' She had practically everything she owned out on the bed but she asked me as though my answer would solve everything for her.

'My jeans,' I said. 'And yes, they're clean.'

'You're not wearing jeans to the exhibition opening.'

'Okay, my denim skirt with that new top. Will

99.

that do?'

'Providing you have a shower and wash that hair.'

'I'm not meeting *my* boyfriend.' I felt obliged to point that out.

'No, but you *are* meeting mine, and I want you to look your best.'

'Do you think he's worrying what he's going to wear?'

'He might be,' she said.

'I doubt it. Boys don't.'

'Some do — when they get over a certain age. What am I going to wear?'

'Your rosebud dress,' I told her and separated it from the pile, 'and the shoes that go with it and I'll subdue your hair for you if you like. You'll be beautiful, Mum.'

'We both look good,' Mum said finally when we were ready to go only half an hour before we needed to be. 'Come on, Millie, I want to get there early anyway, just to make sure everything is looking as good as we are.'

I'd been to the TAFE before, of course, but it all looked different at night and the exhibition had been hung in a gallery space I hadn't seen before. It looked great. There was a table right at the front with a roll of paper on it and a handful of felt-tipped pens so you could write your comments on it. Other tables were covered with white paper which had been sketched on, so when you went to get a biscuit and cheese, you had to reach across someone's face or a bit of a leg or a bent-over tree. Other tables invited you to sketch, with big fat pencils laid out on them along with the dips and baskets of baguettes.

'Hospitality students are catering,' Mum said, looking around the room critically. 'Look, there's the installation I was telling you about.'

In the middle of the room was this kind of forest of things hanging down — from fishing line, I guessed, because you could hardly see what was allowing them to hang in midair like that.

'What are they?'

'Read the title, darling,' Mum said.

'Rev Head Chimes?'

'They're all car bits. He got them from the automotive boys. Great, isn't it? You can walk through it, Millie, and they make noises.'

I walked through it and they did make noises, but not the noises I expected. I heard a car start up, really loudly, and that made me jump. Then something else went *boom boom boom*, just like those too-loud car stereos with too much bass, and a car burglar alarm went off, too.

Mum was watching, laughing her head off.

'It's fantastic, isn't it?' she said. They work on

some kind of light-trigger thing – like automatic doors do. When you walk through it, the sensors pick up your movement and set off the sounds. It's hilarious. Come on, come to my office now and we can worry in there until it's time for people to arrive.'

When we got to her office, there was a big bunch of flowers at the door.

'Oh my,' Mum said, picking them up. 'Oh Millie, look, they're beautiful.'

They were those soft feathery flowers. I can't remember their name but their petals look exactly like some kind of feathers and they feel like them, too. They're Australian, and much artier than plain roses or chrysanthemums. I knew they'd come from *The Boyfriend* before Mum even read out the card.

'Kate. Your night. Celebrate all the hard work. With love, Tom.'

'That's pretty nice of him,' I said grudgingly. I probably wouldn't have to get rid of him. Which was a good thing because I didn't know how you got rid of a boyfriend and Rachel and Helen's suggestions had been funny, wacky and sometimes downright dangerous.

When he turned up, he was nice. He had dark

hair and eyes and a way of looking at Mum that made me feel both really proud of her and as though I was eavesdropping on him looking at her, if you know what I mean.

'You're Millie,' he said, and stuck out his hand for me to shake. That made me feel kind of awkward, because I'm a bit left/right dyslexic and I didn't have my watch on, so for a minute I dithered about which hand I should use. 'You look like Kate.'

'I look like Patrick, too,' I told him. 'I've got Patrick's hair, which is good when it rains because Mum's goes all frizzy at the slightest hint of wet weather, but bad otherwise because curly hair is cool.'

'Right,' he said and looked around the exhibition for help.

'Have you walked through the installation?' I asked him.

'No. Shall we do that together while your mum is swanning around?'

'Okay, but put your fingers in your ears.'

He didn't, of course. It's funny how grown-ups don't ever really take a kid's advice. The noise blasted out and he jumped and then grinned at me.

'Should have had my fingers in my ears,' he said and right away I liked him.

I didn't spend all my time with Tom, of course. Mum's students were there and I met them and walked around some of the night with a couple of them. I was introduced to everyone and couldn't remember anyone's names, but that was okay because no one expected me to. Everyone asked me if I was going to be an artist like Mum, but I told them that she'd taken that slot in our family and I was going to have to choose something else.

I played with Susie's daughter, too. Susie was the coolest of Mum's students. She was dressed in tie-dyed leggings and a series of tie-dyed tops — seriously a series. The bottom one was that kind of mesh stuff and had long sleeves and was all dark purples. The next one was lighter purples and had three-quarter sleeves, still out of the same mesh. The next one had short sleeves and finally, over them all she wore an orange tie-dyed singlet. She had great shoes, too. I always look at shoes because of Mum's soul. Susie's shoes were orange. One of them had a bee painted on it and the other had a flower.

'They're called "You're the Bee's Knees,"' she said, when she saw me looking at them. 'I painted them myself. Do you like them?'

'I love them,' I told her. 'They are the best shoes in this whole room, and that includes my mum's and I thought she was the queen of shoes until I saw yours.'

After the opening we went to a pizza place. My mother and her boyfriend held hands. When I went to the toilet, Mum followed me.

'Would you mind if Tom came home with us tonight?' she asked, looking at me in the mirror's reflection.

'No, that's what he's supposed to do, isn't he?'

'Only if you're comfortable with the idea, Millie.'

'I'll have to get used to it, if you're going to have a boyfriend, Mum,' I pointed out. 'Just so long as he's nicer than Pig's ... I mean, Brendan.'

'Oh Millie, what were you going to call him?'

'Pig's Trotters,' I said. 'Well, he's horrible. I think Mitchell should get rid of him.'

'I think Sheri should get rid of him.' Mum sighed. 'But she makes excuses for him: Brendan's so busy, so caring about other people, so dedicated to his job, so good with those kids. He's not great with Mitchell and it's hard to see where he's caring about her!'

'So Tom'll be there when I wake up in the morning?'

'Tom? Well, yes, I guess. Is that a problem?'

'Only that breakfast is a kind of private thing.'

'We could go out, maybe?' Mum offered. 'Have breakfast at Evita's?'

'Can we talk about it tomorrow?' I yawned. I was suddenly very tired and all I wanted to do was to get home and crawl into my own safe bed with Merlin at the top and Pavlov down the bottom.

'Sure, we can do that, Millie. No breakfast decisions until the morning. Thanks for being a great daughter, though.'

'Thanks for being a great mum,' I said and snuggled into her for a second. She smelt perfumey, like incense but better. 'But you're not the shoe queen anymore. Did you see Susie's shoes?'

'I did,' Mum said. 'I'm thinking of asking her if she'll make me a pair. Will that reinstate me?'

'Would she make me a pair, too?'

'Maybe. But your feet are still growing, Millie, so you'd only have them a short time.'

'I don't care,' I said. 'It would be worth it.'

'We'll see,' Mum said. 'No promises, though. It depends on Susie.'

It was strange hearing Mum and Tom talking in the lounge room. I wasn't used to it. Pavlov growled a bit in her sleep. She wasn't used to it either. It felt a bit like it does before a storm — a change in the air.

CHAPTER TEN

R.H. invited me to go and watch his basketball game! I couldn't believe it. He just strolled across to where Helen-and-Sarah-and-Rachel and I were chucking the ball around and, in front of them, said, 'Hey Millie, I didn't know you played basketball.'

'I don't,' I said. 'We're just mucking around.'

'If you're interested, you should come along to the game on Saturday. We're playing against St Mick's.'

'Are you asking her out?' Rachel asked.

My face felt hot.

'Just to the game,' *R.H.* said, 'if she's interested.'

'Sure, I'd like that,' I answered. My voice

sounded tight and squeaky.

'I have to be at the basketball courts at ten o'clock on Saturday morning,' I told Mum as soon as I got home from school. 'Our school is playing St Mick's.'

'Since when have you wanted to go and watch basketball?' Mum asked. She was sorting through a pile of clothes on the bed.

'Since this boy asked me to go and watch him play,' I said. 'I can go, can't I? It's not a date or anything but I want to go.'

'Well, you'll have to work it out with Tom,' Mum said. 'I have to leave you with him this weekend.'

'What?'

'Some funding came through at the last minute. I'm sorry, Millie, we didn't think it would happen. The application went in late, then it got lost, then they found it and then they decided I should go.'

'Go where?'

'A conference in Canberra. It's a great opportunity. I simply can't knock it back, Millie. Tom said he wouldn't mind looking after you. Can you cope with that?'

'I guess. So long as he takes me to the basketball game.'

I liked Tom even if he didn't do the stuff that everyone said boyfriends did. He hadn't bought me a television for my room. He never gave me extra pocket money or bought lollies for me or slyly passed me a ten-dollar note to go and spend at the shopping centre so he and Mum could have time together.

He just kind of hung around. He took photos a lot. Which you'd expect, I suppose, as that was what he did. Sometimes he and Mum planned a day somewhere, like Lake Glenmaggie, taking photographs and painting, and Pavlov and I went with them, being sure to remember a book and lots of food because it could get kind of boring. Mum offered to buy me a sketchbook and charcoal or pastels, but she was our family's artist, not me.

Sometimes we went back to Tom's place and watched while he developed the photographs in his darkroom. That was really exciting. You put this blank paper in the developing tank and just watched while the picture slowly floated to the surface of the paper. It was like magic. Then I got to peg them up carefully on the little line that was strung at one end of the darkroom.

You couldn't go in the darkroom if the little red light was on because you might ruin all the photos. You had to knock then, to make sure that Tom wasn't in the middle of exposing them, when any extra light could mean disaster. He'd prefer his tea cold rather than risk losing photographs.

'I'm sure he'll take you to the basketball game. I'll ask him for you, okay? Look, Millie, do you think that this top would be all right with those trousers? Because then I can just take that skirt which does go with that top.'

The phone rang before I could answer her.

'Hello,' I said. 'Millie here.'

'Hello, darling, how are you?'

'Patrick! Mum, it's Patrick! Yes, I'm fine, we're all fine … You're what? … Mum, Patrick's coming to Sydney!'

'He's what?' Mum snatched the phone from me. 'When are you in Sydney, Patrick?'

'Give me the phone back, Mum! I was talking to him first.'

'Hold on for a sec, can you? Millie, just give me some time, okay. Then you can talk to him again. Patrick, how long are you over for? Are we going to see you? Oh, what a shame. No, I'll be in Canberra. Millie? No, she's staying with … just hold on.'

Mum took the phone in to her bedroom, giving me a warning look I couldn't misread. I had to wait my turn and I might as well be patient.

It was so unfair. Patrick was going to Sydney only – a science conference. Then he had to go straight back to England to start teaching again.

'I can't help it,' he said, his voice all warm and

close on the phone. 'They won't give me leave, Millie. I've a full teaching load. It'll be lucky if your mum can come to Sydney after her conference.'

'When will *I* see you?'

'I'll be back for Christmas this year, definitely. I couldn't go for two years in a row without seeing my Millie. Now, tell me, how are things? What is this Tom like?'

'It's so unfair,' I said to Mum. 'He's my father. He isn't even related to you but you get to see him and I don't.'

'You can write him a long letter,' Mum said, 'and I can give it to him — that is, if Tom can mind you the extra day.'

'I can email him if I want to,' I pointed out, snappish.

'Why don't we get Tom to take some photos of you and Pavlov and I'll take them up with me?'

'Okay.' It didn't help that much but it was better than nothing, and Patrick had promised that this Christmas — which was ages away of course — he'd come back to Australia come hell or high water. That's exactly what he said: 'come hell or high water'. I liked the sound of that.

Tom came around the next afternoon and took photos of us, and Mum too. He fussed around with lights and reflections and Mum fussed around with make-up, scarves and even a hat.

'It's not for Patrick,' she told Tom. 'If I look okay in any of these and not like someone with early-onset dementia, I'll use them for the next show catalogue. If you don't mind.'

'Of course I don't mind, Kate. I'd be flattered. And I'm really happy to take shots of Millie for her dad to see, and to mind her for the extra time. Honestly, I'm delighted to be able to do that. It's just ... I just feel ... I know you're good friends and that's important. It's just that I feel ...'

'It's okay.' Mum went up and gave him a hug, awkwardly because he had cameras dangling around his neck. 'It's okay, Tom. We'll talk later.'

Why do adults do that? I wasn't stupid. I knew that Tom didn't want to think about Mum meeting Patrick in Sydney, because they might fall into each other's arms again after all these years and discover they really truly loved each other. As if.

I wanted to tell him that Mum and Patrick weren't like that. As he took our photos he looked as if he was trying very hard not to be miserable. Mum did her best, but she was too excited about the conference and about seeing Patrick so she constantly put her foot in it.

We went over to Tom's to have dinner so he could develop the photos in the dark room. Mum bought take-away pizza. I waited until Tom was ready to do the developing and then asked if I could help.

'Sure,' he said, 'come on in. I can always use an assistant.'

While I jiggled photos around and peered through the enlarger and hung up the prints on the little clothes line, I told Tom about Patrick.

'You know, you're *The Boyfriend*,' I said to Tom, 'not Patrick. I mean, Mum does love him, of course. Because they are the best friends in the world. But it's that friends kind of love, not the smoochy kind.'

'I know,' Tom said, in an unconvinced voice 'It's fine. Honestly. And we'll have a good time together, I'm sure. We'll keep the fort for your mum.'

When we got home later, with ten beautiful black and white photographs that made both Mum and me look like long-ago movie stars, I said to Mum, 'He's nice, Tom, even if he is *The Boyfriend*. I like him, you know.'

'Mmm,' Mum said. 'So do I, Millie.'

'You'll ring him, won't you, when you're away?'

'Well, of course I will.'

'It's just that sometimes you forget, you know. Like that time you and Sheri went to Queenscliff and didn't ring May for three days?'

'Oh Millie, that was different. Sheri and I were having a holiday. Or trying to. Honestly, the way May carried on you would have thought I'd abandoned you. Three days, that's all. The nearest public phone wasn't working. I told her that.'

'I didn't mean you to go over it all again,' I said. 'It's just that I think you'll have to ring Tom, that's all.'

'Tom's old enough to look after himself. You're the one I have to ring.' And Mum gave me a quick grin.

'And Tom,' I insisted. 'And take your mobile, Mum. I mean it. Don't forget *it* again either.'

Mum's mobile was the most immobile cell phone in the world. It often lived on the top of the bookshelf closest to the front door. It was there so she'd see it before she left the house. The trouble was, Mum was always leaving the house in a mad rush and the mobile stayed put.

'I'll take my mobile. Of course, I'll take my mobile,' Mum said crossly. 'Honestly, Millie, that's why people have them. I'm not stupid.'

Getting Mum packed and off was a major exercise. Without Sheri, Mum needed my help with her clothes. I wasn't the best person in the world to ask. But I was better than Tom, who said that everything looked terrific when even I could see that the brown skirt was shiny at the back and that her new impulse-buy trousers made her bum look enormous.

'Didn't you look in the mirror?' I asked her.

'Of course I did, but I looked at the front, not the back. I didn't have time to look at the back. I don't think it can look that big, Millie. I think you're exaggerating. It's just my bottom, that's all. It's no bigger than ever it has been.'

'Well, it looks huge in those trousers, but if you want to wear them, go ahead.'

I was worried enough about my own clothes. I had to go to Rowan's basketball game on Saturday and I had nothing to wear.

I had to start calling him Rowan, I decided, not just *R.H.* I couldn't turn up on Saturday and call him by his initials. He would think that was very peculiar. I had some practice at school.

Tayla came over while Helen-Rachel-and-I were having lunch (Sarah was sick).

'I hear you're going out with Rowan,' she said, standing directly in front of me, her arms crossed and her runners (new) planted firmly, as though she was ready for some kind of action.

'I'm not,' I said.

'She is,' Helen-and-Rachel said.

'I suggest you back off,' Tayla said. 'He asked me out first and just because I said no this time doesn't mean that I'll say no next time. So, if you don't want trouble, Miss Dilly Millie, I'd make

115.

sure that it doesn't happen again.'

'You've got no right to intimidate her,' Helen said. 'Millie can go out with Rowan if she wants to.'

'That's right,' Rachel said, 'so long as he wants to, too. Who do you think you are, Tayla?'

Tayla looked at Rachel as though Rachel was a particularly unpleasant bug she'd found on her sandwich. 'Who do I think I am? Well, for your information, Rachel, I know who I am and that's one hell of a lot skinnier and prettier than you are, so I'd pull my head in if I were you, Lard Bum.'

'Who're you calling Lard Bum?' Rachel asked, getting up.

'Do you really have to ask?' Tayla turned away from Rachel and back to me. 'So did you hear what I said, Millie, or do your friends have to speak for you?'

'I heard.' Inside me my heart was beating out of control. Had Rowan really asked Tayla to the game first? Was I just his second-best choice? I didn't even know that. I could have been his third- or fourth- or even fifth-best choice. How would I know? I could hardly ask every girl in our grade whether or not she'd been asked first.

'Good.' Tayla strolled away casually, her skirt flipping as she walked.

'She's horrible,' Helen said. 'You haven't got a

huge bum, Rachel, so don't look like that.'

'I don't care anyway,' Rachel said. 'It's my bum and I like it.'

'Do you really think he asked her out first?'

Helen and Rachel looked at each other. They didn't mean to, I knew that. It was the kind of look you almost can't stop happening — the checking-up look.

'I don't really know,' Helen said.

'I think he might have,' Rachel said at the same time.

'So he only wants me to go because she's said no?'

'He really likes you, Millie, otherwise he wouldn't have thought of you at all.' Helen patted my arm.

'Anyway,' Rachel said, 'that's not really important. The thing is that he did ask you and you'll be at the game, not Miss Cat's Bum Mouth. You'll be there. That's what counts.'

That night I wrote in my journal:

To the Spirit of Justice and Everything
that is Fair, please let something happen
to Tayla Cameron. Let her get a really bad
pimple right on her nose or in the middle
of her forehead. Let it be big and bright

red and unsqueezable. Let it get bigger and bigger until she's almost scared to squeeze it in case it explodes. Let it be the biggest pimple in the world and horrible to look at.

I ask this because Tayla Cameron's soul is like that. Big and horrible. I know it's against the rules to ask for bad things to happen,

but she really does deserve it.

Your servant,

Millie.

I didn't expect the Spirit to do anything, really. Helen was right, it had too much to do anyway, what with all the starvation and war and cancer in the world. But you never knew, and if anyone deserved a huge pimple somewhere where everyone could see it, it was Tayla Cameron. Nothing was surer.

CHAPTER ELEVEN

The Spirit of Justice was clearly not listening, or was not very good at its job. I got the pimple. I woke up with it on Friday. It wasn't on my nose or my forehead. It was on my chin, which was just as bad. It was huge, bright red and totally unsqueezable. I know, because I tried for ten minutes.

'Millie, get out of the bathroom. I need to get ready to go to Canberra. What are you doing in there?'

'Nothing.'

'Well, stop hogging it, then. Honestly, I don't know what's got into you. I can remember when I had to beg you to have a shower. Now you're in the bathroom all the time. I've got to get ready.'

'I heard you. I'll be out in a minute.'

I couldn't believe the pimple. It pulsated, honest. I tried to cover it up with some of Kate's liquid foundation No. 5, but that just made it go kind of scaly on top. It didn't seem to diminish the glaring red at all.

'Millie, I'm counting to ten.'

'Okay, okay. God, you'd think it was a crime getting ready for school. You'd think you wanted me to go to school dirty and stinking with knots in my hair.'

Mum was tapping her foot when I got out of the bathroom. She looked me up and down carefully but I had my hand over the lower part of my face.

'What's wrong with your chin?'

'Nothing.'

'Well, why are you holding it like that?'

'I'm not. It's just comfortable this way, that's all.'

'Millie, come on, let me see.'

Reluctantly I moved my hand.

'I don't see anything,' Mum said. 'What's wrong?'

'I've got a huge pimple, Mum. Look! The basketball game is tomorrow and it won't go away for that. It's my own fault. I asked that Tayla Cameron get a pimple, not me, but it backfired.'

'What backfired? Who's Tayla Cameron? I can't see a *huge* pimple, just a pretty ordinary-sized one.'

'Oh Mum, you're hopeless.' I stalked off to my room. For an artist Mum was remarkably unobservant, particularly when it came to her own daughter. I wished for one minute — okay, maybe for five minutes — that I had a beautician for a mother. Someone who would look at my face and really see it in all its horribleness and then suggest something practical that I could do about it. Instead I had a mother who shrugged off acne as though it was nothing, like having to have stale bread sandwiches for lunch, which I hated too, but which, I had to admit, didn't happen that often and wasn't as bad as pimples anyway. Or at least not as bad as this pimple. Rowan would take one look at it on my chin and never want to come near me again. I would die of a broken heart.

Mum came out of the bathroom. She looked kind of nervy but great. She was wearing a new dark purple skirt and a shirt that swirled around with colour and made me think of dancing. 'Millie, you must listen to this. Here's where I'm staying in Canberra. Stick it up on the noticeboard, will you, and highlight the phone number. I'll be leaving there Sunday night and leaving Sydney on Monday afternoon, after I've seen Patrick.'

'You've got a mobile phone, Mum. I don't need all these numbers.'

'You do. What happens if my mobile battery runs out?'

'You packed your charger, didn't you?'

'Of course I did. Accidents can happen though, or it might be stolen. These are back-up numbers, Millie. Stick them up now. There's frozen food: a curry, two lots of pasta sauce and some lasagne. I don't want Tom to have to cook for you both, so remind him, will you? And, Millie, don't hassle him, okay? Don't ask for Maccas or pizza or anything like that. Remember he's doing me a huge favour. We haven't even been going out for long. Not many men would take on minding a child.'

'He's *The Boyfriend*,' I said to her crossly. I don't like being called a child. 'He's just doing it so he won't be sacked.'

'He's not,' Mum said. 'He's doing it to help out. And it is helping, Millie, so you be good. Don't be sarcastic with him. He hasn't had much to do with kids. Please, Millie. Treat him gently, huh?'

'Okay, I will. But you bring me back something, Mum, because I won't even get to see Patrick.'

'Millie!'

'Well, it's true.'

'You know Patrick would do anything to see you. He simply has to get back to teach, Millie. I'll hardly see him. He's the keynote speaker at his conference. We should both be really proud of him. But it doesn't mean that you automatically get something.'

'I need a new journal,' I said, ignoring her. 'I bet you could get something really cool like that at the Gallery. You are going to the Gallery, aren't you?'

'Yes, of course. I'm not promising anything, Millie. You don't just get things because I have to go away, but I'll keep it in mind that a new journal would be desirable. Fair enough.'

'Thanks, Mum. You're the best. Don't worry about Tom and me. We'll be fine. I'll look after him for you. I won't forget the food in the freezer and I won't hassle about take-aways. But you have to remind him about the basketball game.'

'Deal.'

I went off to school knowing that when I got home Mum wouldn't be there and Tom would.

'How was school?' he asked. 'Do you want a tea or a coffee?'

'I don't drink coffee,' I said, 'but I'll have a raspberry and peach herbal tea, please.'

'Good, good. Where are they?'

'The tea's all up here, in this cupboard. Cups are down there. Mum keeps coffee in the freezer. Do you know how to work the coffee maker?'

'No.' He looked a bit miserable, as though all the details were a little overwhelming.

'I can show you,' I said. I felt as though I should pat his arm. He just gangled in the kitchen, looking out of place. 'Mum left us dinner, too. In the freezer. We just nuke it in the nuker.'

'Oh,' Tom said, 'I thought we'd just have noodles tonight. Would that be all right with you?'

'Mum said we weren't to have take-aways.'

'Did she? She didn't say that to me.' Tom looked worried. 'Are you allergic to things. She didn't mention anything like that.'

'No. I never get sick. I think it might be *Boyfriend* rules.'

'Oh, is that all it is? So we can have noodles?'

'Tonight we could,' I told him, 'but we'd better eat some of the meals she's frozen. After all, she went to all that trouble for you, you know.'

'We'll make sure we eat something for lunch tomorrow. I just think I have to study this nuker of yours. I'm not up on microwaves. I don't actually have one myself. I'm afraid I'm strictly a chops and three veg kind of man — with take-aways. I do a good line in take-aways. I know all the best places.' He grinned at me.

He must have been a regular at the noodle eatery because they didn't even ask him what he wanted. Just smiled at me and asked me what I'd have.

124.

'This is your girlfriend's daughter?' the woman asked.

'Yes,' he said. 'This is Millie. Millie, this is Ying.'

'Hello,' we both said at once.

'Take a packet of prawn crackers,' Ying said when she handed Tom our order. You only got prawn crackers if you spent over $25 and we'd only spent $17.60. I knew because I added it up.

'Gee, thanks Ying. We'll enjoy those, won't we, Millie?'

'Yes, thank you.'

We ate in front of the television, straight from the noodle boxes, to save on the washing up. We both used forks, though, not the little chopsticks that came with the noodles. For dessert, Tom brought out a family-size block of chocolate, the kind that has lots of fillings, not just the one flavour.

'I like a bit of chocolate,' he said apologetically.

'I shouldn't eat it,' I said. 'I've got this pimple on my chin. And I have to watch Rowan play basketball tomorrow. Mum did tell you, didn't she?'

'Yes, she mentioned that. I have to take you there, right? I can't really see much of a pimple, Millie. I think it would be safe to have a bit.'

We ate the whole block between us and neither of us felt even a little bit sick. I didn't bother telling

125.

Mum about either the noodles or the chocolate when she rang and I noticed Tom didn't either.

The basketball game started at ten o'clock, so naturally I was out of bed, showered and ready by quarter to nine. I decided, after much soul-searching, to wear jeans with a pale blue hippy kind of top. I put lip gloss on, and then I wiped it off again. I didn't want to look as though I was trying too hard.

Tom still hadn't emerged by eight-fifty, so I made coffee. I hoped the smell of it would coax him out. I made it in Mum's expresso machine and I made it extra strong so the smell wafted down the hallway. It worked. He came out of Mum's bedroom at eight-fifty-eight.

'Smells fantastic,' he said, sniffing the air the way Pavlov does when there's something dead nearby.

'Coffee,' I said unnecessarily, and added, 'Basketball's on at ten.'

'Ah, yes.' Tom ran his fingers through his hair. 'How's the pimple?'

'Gone! Must have been the chocolate.'

'Well, then, let's have breakfast and be off.'

We were just about to leave, after crumpets and honey, when the phone rang.

'Just leave it,' I said desperately. 'The machine will pick it up.'

'It might be important.' Tom hovered over the phone.

'Nuh, it won't be. Come on, I'll be late.'

'I have to answer it, Millie. It might be your mum. Hello? Oh, Kate. Hi.'

'Tom!'

'Can I ring you back, Kate? It's just that Millie's got this ... Oh, okay. Sure. Fire away.'

He turned his back to me. I stayed in the room, though, tapping my foot. Not that he could hear that, because the carpet muffled the sound. I watched the digital clock on the mantle click the numbers up, closer and closer to ten o'clock. Rowan would think I wasn't coming. Rowan would think I was unreliable and unpunctual. Rowan would know I wasn't coming and would probably put his basketball bag next to someone else, a girl, a girl whose brother was playing for the other team.

She'd have long curly hair and her skin would be as clear as the morning. She'd like him straightaway. Well, who wouldn't? Rowan had the best smile in the world. It made you feel everything was going to be okay, despite people starving in many countries. It was the kind of smile that made you skip, without even knowing that was what you were doing.

When Tom finally got off the phone I glared at him.

'We may as well not go now,' I said, in my most sarcastic voice, 'the first half will be over.'

'I'm sorry, Millie, but your mother had something rather important to discuss.'

Tom's voice sounded odd.

'So are we going now?' I asked, as he seemed to be just standing in the hallway, as though he meant to stand there forever.

'I thought you didn't want to go now.'

'I was being sarcastic.' Where were *The Boyfriend's* brains?

'Oh, sorry.'

We drove to the basketball courts in silence.

'So can you come and get me at midday?' I asked him when I got out. I was scanning the onlookers, but I couldn't see Rowan anywhere. My heart was thumping and my stomach had butterflies whirling around in it.

'I'll just wait here, I think,' Tom said. 'I've bought my camera. I might try to get some shots.'

I didn't think that was too cool, but when I looked, there were parents sitting around everywhere.

I slowly walked over to the seats. I'd seen Rowan. He was shooting. I didn't want to wave or distract him from that, so I just sat down.

'Well, hello,' a voice behind trilled. 'Fancy you being here, Millie Dillie.'

128.

It was Tayla. I knew even before I turned around.

'What are you doing here?'

'Watching the game, of course. I got here on time.'

'So?'

'Rowan's done really well. They're winning.'

The whistle sounded for half-time. I didn't know whether to go down and see Rowan or not. He looked up and half-waved, but before I could do anything Tayla was running down to him. I stayed where I was. I felt sick. She stayed down with the players even while the coach talked to them. I hated her.

Then the whistle sounded and they were back on.

At the end of the game, Rowan came up to where I was sitting.

'You were late,' he said.

'I couldn't help it,' I told him. 'Mum rang *The Boyfriend* just as we were about to leave and they talked on the phone for hours. You're playing really well, Rowan.'

'You're fantastic,' Tayla gushed from behind. 'You should go for the state team.'

Rowan shrugged but he smiled at Tayla, too. Couldn't he hear how false she was?

'Dad said I could invite you guys back to our

house after the game,' Tayla continued. 'Want to come? We've got a brand new pool table in the games room and we're allowed to play whenever we want.'

'Sure,' Rowan said, 'I'll be in it. What about you, Millie?'

The whole afternoon at Tayla's? I didn't think so. On the other hand, if I didn't go, Tayla and Rowan might end up going out together. What was worse? Tayla for a whole afternoon or Rowan for never?

'I'll have to ask *The Boyfriend*,' I said.

'Go and ask now,' Tayla said, 'because I have to tell Dad whether you're coming or not so he can organise lunch.' She held up a mobile phone. It was pearly pink and matched her tracksuit.

'Gee, is that yours?' Rowan said. 'Lucky you.'

'Well, of course it's mine. It's cool, isn't it?'

'Girlie colour.'

'That's because I'm a girl, dipstick.' Tayla's laugh was high-pitched and evil, although I think she thought it was flirty and cute. I hated Tayla more than I hated boiled parsnip.

'I'll go and ask now,' I said. 'Coming, Rowan?'

'It's got games on it,' Tayla said. 'Want to try one?'

'Sure.' He took the phone from Tayla.

I'd lost him to a mobile phone game.

I walked over to the car. Tom was reading.

'How's it going?'

'Okay,' he said. 'What are you up to?'

'I'm supposed to be asking you if I can go to Tayla's house this afternoon.' I looked over to where Tayla and Rowan were standing. She had her hand on his shoulder.

'I thought you had a project to do?'

'Yeah, I forgot that. Good. I couldn't decide if it was going to be worse than being in a pit of stinging scorpions anyway.'

'Is this a friend of yours?'

'No, I hate her.'

'Of course, I should have known.' Tom smiled at me but his eyes looked sad.

'Hey,' I said, 'I'm sorry about this morning.'

'That's okay, Millie. I'm sorry the call took so long. Your Mum ...' He trailed off, looking past me.

'Yeah?'

'Oh, just that your mum wants to stay an extra couple of days in Sydney. She said Patrick had managed to get two evenings off from conference stuff. Apparently he knows someone there who owns a gallery and he's arranged a dinner for them both. She said that she wouldn't do it if it was going to be inconvenient but it did sound like a wonderful opportunity.'

'Then why do you sound so miserable?' I hadn't

meant to say that. It just came out because he did look so gloomy.

'I'm not,' Tom said firmly, 'not at all. It's a terrific chance for her to catch up with your dad and meet people who might help her in her career. I don't think there's anything more to it than that.'

'Tayla's after Rowan,' I said, 'and she's going to get him because she's got a new pool table and a pink mobile phone with games on it.'

Tom looked at me and blinked. I could feel my chin wobble.

'I don't even think I want to say goodbye,' I said. 'I think we could just go home now.'

Tom took me to a café for lunch. He bought me a lime spider and a toasted chicken foccacia. He passed me paper napkins when I cried and he listened to the whole story.

'And I've got this stupid project to do and I don't know anything about this place, nothing at all. We haven't even lived here long enough. How am I supposed to know about it? So when is Mum coming home?'

'Thursday, she said.' Tom sounded gloomy again.

'That's a whole extra four days!'

'Three days, really.'

We went home but we couldn't settle down to anything. I kept thinking about Rowan reaching out for Tayla's mobile phone. They'd be playing pool together. She'd be giggling and telling Rowan how wonderful he was. It was sick-making. Tom seemed to mope around, too, picking up his book, reading a page, staring out into space, re-reading the page and sighing.

I was trying to brainstorm ideas for my project. Brainstorming is where you write everything down, even the most stupid ideas. I had only stupid ideas.

My Environment - What I Love, What I Hate

I love the TAFE restaurant, not that I've
   been more than once, and the wood-fired
pizza place. I hate days when the smell of
the paper mill drifts into town and it rains.
  I hate the kids hanging around the mall.
I love the mountains and the clouds. I hate
   Tayla. I really really hate Tayla. And Rowan
for liking her. I hate Rowan almost as much
   as I hate Tayla. But not quite as much,
because he's still got that smile. I hate the
   fact that I didn't go back to Tayla's, but
   it would have been worse, going back.
Decisions like that stink. I hate broken
hearts.
  My heart is broken.

'I think I'll take Pavlov for a walk. Want to come?'

'Sure, I'd love that,' Tom said. 'It would be good to get out, away from the demons in my head.'

'You have demons in your head?'

'Sort of.'

'So do I. What are yours saying?'

'Just stupid stuff,' Tom said, 'nothing important. And yours?'

'Mine are telling me that Tayla is leaning over Rowan right at this moment and giggling at him, and he's smiling at her the way he does that makes his whole face glow at you and he's smiling like that for her, not for me. I should have gone back with them, but if I had it would have been awful. It would have been awful going back and it's awful imagining what's going on, too. Do you know what I mean?'

'Yes,' Tom said. 'Yes, I know absolutely what you mean.'

'Have you had a broken heart?'

'Oh, once or twice.'

'How long did it take you to get over it?'

'It seemed to take forever but gradually I felt better. The second time was worse.'

'This is my first ever. How long did it take you the first time?'

'I'm not sure,' Tom said, 'but do you want to know what really helped?'

'Yes.'

'Pizza and videos. What do you reckon?'

'What about Mum's frozen dinners?'

'We've got three extra days to eat them now.' Tom didn't sound thrilled at the idea.

'Mum's a good cook,' I told him. 'They'll be yummy.'

'It's not that,' Tom said, 'and it isn't you, either, Millie. I'm enjoying your company, broken-hearted and all. Where are we going?'

'Up to the reserve,' I told him. 'There's a little lake and birds and we can let Pavlov off, even though the sign says you can't. He never chases the birds.'

'This is pretty,' Tom commented, when we got there. 'It's been ages since I've been here.'

'I like it,' I said, 'because of the birds. I like the moor hens.'

'Yes, the purple ones are spectacular, aren't they? Wish I'd brought my camera.'

'If you could be any kind of bird at all, what sort would you be?' I asked Tom, as we walked Pavlov around the lake.

'Oh, I think I'd be an owl,' he said. 'Yes, definitely an owl. What about you?'

I was wishing I'd thought of an owl. That was

a good answer. Owls are powerful and wise, good hunters, and I love their round, surprised faces.

'I'll have to think about it.'

'Or a phoenix. Now that would be the bird to be, rising again and again out of the flames.'

'You can't be something mythic,' I said rather snappily. 'You have to be a real bird.'

When we got home from the walk I looked kookaburras up on the Internet. I wanted to get the facts right.

'I'm a kookaburra,' I told Tom that evening when we went out for pizza. 'They are quite long-lived for birds, you know, and they mate for life. They laugh to mark their boundaries and their young don't move totally away from home but help to raise the next brood.'

'They're great birds,' Tom said, 'but I still want to be an owl.'

'I want to be something that mates for life. It just sounds so much simpler. Do owls mate for life?'

'I'm not sure, but you're right, it would be much simpler if we could all do that. Except then I wouldn't have met your mum, would I?'

'But you wouldn't have had your heart broken, either. Think of that.'

'It didn't do me any harm, really. Probably helped grow me up a bit. There's a persuasive theory, Millie, that men don't really grow up until they're in their thirties.'

'Looks like I'll have to settle for a boy, then,' I said. It was only just possible to imagine being twenty. Anything older was out of my imagination's range.

Tom laughed and patted my head.

'You'll grow him up, Millie. You'll be all right.'

I wrote that down in my journal later, exactly what Tom had said. It was the best thing anyone had said to me all week.

CHAPTER TWELVE

I woke up with the nagging kind of feeling that something was wrong. I checked everything I could think of. Aliens hadn't abducted me (a scientist's daughter shouldn't believe in aliens, but I still do). Pavlov lay on the end of my bed, so it wasn't Pavlov. I lifted the edge of the blind and looked out. The little yellow-winged honey eater flew off. All was well with the world – the new ice age hadn't come.

Then I remembered The Project. Today was D-Day. Desperation Day. It was due in tomorrow and all I had was a crummy bit of stupid brainstorming, which was more about Rowan than the project topic.

'I've got to do my project,' I yelled through Tom's closed door. 'Tom, I've got to do my project.'

'Hang on, Millie, it's only 7.30. It's Sunday, for heaven's sake. Haven't you heard of the day of rest?'

'This is a crisis, Tom.'

'Millie, it's too early for a crisis.'

'I'll make coffee,' I offered.

'I suppose I won't get back to sleep. All right, make coffee.'

I did extra special coffee, heating the milk and sprinkling chocolate over the top, just like they do in a café.

'Brilliant,' Tom said, taking a sip. 'Where did you learn this, Millie?'

'The project,' I said, sitting down opposite him. 'Tom, it's the last day. It's due tomorrow. I'll fail.'

'Why have you left it up until now? Couldn't you have sorted this out with your mother? I don't know anything about school projects.'

'I didn't mention it to Mum. I was trying to avoid it.'

'But why, Millie? Why leave it to the last minute?'

'You mean, why leave it until you're here.'

'Well, yes, I suppose I do mean that. School projects are way out of my field of experience. You

139.

should have brought this up with Kate.'

'I know. I'm really sorry, Tom. This is way outside a boyfriend's responsibility.'

Tom sighed. 'You'd better tell me anyway.'

I told him everything. I even showed him my brainstorming, although normally I wouldn't have done that because it was so pathetic, but I needed Tom to see how dire the situation was.

'Yes,' he said after I explained. 'Yes, I can see it isn't good.'

We sat for a while in silence. Finally he said, 'You know that little park you took me to yesterday?'

'What's that got to do with The Project?' I asked. Sometimes *The Boyfriend* was exasperating.

'Just humour me here,' Tom said, smiling at me.

'If you say so.'

'You like going there, don't you?'

'Of course.'

'Why?'

'Because of the birds. You know that.'

'Ah, the birds. Birds seem to be a bit special to you, aren't they?'

'Not until we came here,' I started, and then stopped. 'Oh.'

Tom nodded, clearly pleased with himself. 'So what I'm thinking,' he said, 'and honestly, Millie, this is my only suggestion. If you don't want to do this, you'll have to work out what you can do by yourself, okay?'

'It sounds great already,' I said.

'You haven't heard me yet.' Tom looked at me and shook his head, 'So, we go to this place I know, a proper wetlands reserve, with the camera gear. You can use my digital camera and one of the 35 mm cameras. We'll take tripods. We'll get your project done the only way I know how. And it will be fun, or it could be. How does that sound?'

We spent the whole morning at the wetlands. Tom showed me how to use his digi camera, how to mount it on the tripod, how to use the menu and the zoom. He let me take a roll of film on one of his 35 mm cameras. He took photos, too – some of the birds, some of me and some of Pavlov. I could tell when he was happy because he'd make this little chuckly sound, or say, 'Well, well,' in a pleased voice.

We got home really hungry and finally nuked one of Mum's frozen dinners. It was really a dinner dinner but we were so hungry that Tom said it didn't matter. He got everything together to take to his place, while I set the table and made him more coffee.

When we got to his place, after lunch, Tom said, 'You've helped me before, but you haven't done it from the beginning, have you?'

I shook my head.

'First thing you have to do is to rewind your film, but not so far the film strip goes right back into the cannister, because then we'll have to open the cannister with a bottle opener, which is a pain in the ...'

'Bum,' I supplied helpfully.

'Right. So press that little button in and rotate that lever. When you feel the slightest resistance, you have to stop.'

'You mean me? I have to do it?'

'Of course, Millie, it's your project. You're going to do everything.'

'What if I get it wrong?'

'Well, if you get this bit wrong, we'll just open the cannister with a bottle opener. You won't get it wrong though. You'll be fine.'

I didn't get it wrong. I didn't get anything wrong. I did exactly what Tom told me to do and I did everything as carefully as if I were a scientist working in a laboratory.

I mixed up the developer and agitated the developing tank. Then I fixed the negatives. I washed and washed the film and rinsed it with wetting agent so there wouldn't be any marks from the water drying. Finally we hung the negatives on the little line to dry. We did three rolls of film like that.

While the film dried, we downloaded the digi photos on to Tom's computer.

'There's procedure and method here, too,' Tom said. 'You've got to be really methodical about photography. It's 5 percent inspiration, 15 percent timing and 80 percent method. I think that's so with all art, really.'

We looked at my photos, one by one.

'Well, well,' Tom said about some of them, and I knew they were the ones he particularly liked.

I loved nearly all of them, even the ones that were fuzzily out of focus. There was one of a big pelican opening his beak really wide, and another shot of him fluffing up his wings. There was one of a pair of little Eurasian coots floating on water so smooth it looked as though they were floating on the reflected clouds. There was even a great photo of Tom, one of my sneaky ones, looking just the way he looked before he began to smile at you. He looked startled at the photos of himself.

'Good heavens!' he said, 'do I really look like that?'

'A lot of the time,' I told him. 'But it's a good look, Tom. See all those little creasy lines near your eyes? When you smile, they go up and make you look user-friendly.'

'I didn't realise there were quite so many creasy lines,' Tom said.

'But they're good. They make you look soft.'

'Well, well,' he said with one of his chuckly noises. 'Soft, eh? You know, Millie, I think you've got a good eye for photography.'

We printed out the best of my bird photographs, the best sneaky shot of Tom and one of the primeval swamp-dog photos of Pavlov.

'Now for the exciting bit,' Tom said. 'I bet that film is dry by now.'

We could only do black-and-white photos, of course, but I like them. They look like the proper photographs in books.

First we did a contact print, a sheet of all the photographs printed up exactly the same size as the negatives. That was so we could tell which negatives we wanted to enlarge.

We took our contact sheets out into the lounge room to look at over a cup of coffee (instant) for Tom and a glass of juice for me. It was funny – some of the shots I could remember thinking would be really fantastic weren't particularly good and others surprised me.

'How many can I do?'

'Well, we've got some time constraints,' Tom said, 'but I reckon you could do at least three for the project. We can always print up more another day. How does that sound?'

It was really hard choosing. I knew they had to

be project photos, but there was a great one of Tom.

'Could I do that later? Before Mum comes home? I know she'd really like it. It looks like a proper portrait.'

Tom squinted at it through the magnifying glass. He had one specifically for looking at contact prints.

'You don't think it makes me look old?'

'No, you look great. It will be a kind of record of what we did when she was away. She'd like that.'

'Yeah, it is good,' Tom said. 'Maybe we'll have a go at it tomorrow night. But today it's the project. Professional photographers have to prioritise, too, you know. Suppose you're out taking photos of … someone's racehorse … and you see this great old farmer sitting around. When you get home, you have to do the horse first, even if you think the farmer's a better photograph. The horse is your bread and butter.'

We marked the photographs I wanted to enlarge with a special pen and then went back into the darkroom.

Enlarging was the most fun. I'd watched some of that before but I hadn't done it myself. It was totally awesome. The blank paper went into the tray, and while we watched, the image floated magically on to the paper.

The prints looked great. When I saw them all

hanging on the line drying, it was as though they no longer were my photos but just real photographs, taken by someone who knew what they were doing.

'That's my favourite,' Tom said. 'I like the composition of that one. The tree in the foreground leads your eye to the group of herons, but they aren't in the middle of the photograph. A lot of new photographers put their subject matter bang in the middle of the photograph, but you're better off doing what you've done – dividing the image into threes.'

'Can you take photos at night?' I asked. 'That would be so cool, to have a couple of shots of the same place tonight.'

Tom laughed. 'Well, not really,' he said. 'You wouldn't see anything at night. But' – he checked his watch – 'it's earlier than I thought it would be. We could go back for some late-afternoon shots, if you like. You might get some sunset shots. That's if you're really keen?'

'I am.'

'What about your project? There's more to it than photographs.'

'I can do the information on your computer. I'll write it up and print it out here. I can do that while the negs are drying.'

I liked saying 'negs', the way Tom did, casually.

'You could, I guess,' Tom said. 'You'd just squeak it in. Then you'll have to mount the photographs.'

'Black card. There's two big pieces under Mum's bed. We used it last year for these really neat Christmas cards.'

'I've got some special rubber glue you can use. It won't damage the photos. That way you can just unpeel them when the project's been marked and we can get a couple of the photographs framed, I reckon. They'll look good on the wall of your bedroom.'

There were new birds at the wetlands when we got back. Tom said perhaps they came out only in the evening. They had longish legs, not as long as heron legs, but long for their small bodies, and they were cheep-cheepy.

'What are they?'

'I don't know.' Tom frowned. 'I kind of want to say sandpipers but I don't see how they can be. I thought sandpipers were ocean birds. I could be wrong, though. Birds aren't my specialty. I know the obvious ones, that's all.'

I got a couple of sunset shots with the cheepy birds in, although they weren't exactly close. It was getting dark by the time we packed up all the gear. We were walking back to the car when a strange bird flew over us.

'That's one I do know,' Tom said, turning to

watch it.

'I don't. I've never seen it before. What is it?' Birds being my specialty I thought I should know.

'Ah ha. I tell you what, Millie. You find it in the bird book at home and I'll give you something special. Remember how it flies. That's your biggest clue.'

'It was all hunkered in on itself.'

'That's right.' Tom sounded pleased, although I couldn't see his face in the dark. 'They fly as if they haven't got a neck. Remember that.'

I had to type up all the project information before I looked at Tom's bird book. That was prioritising. The book sat on his desk and called me, but I ignored it.

'It'll be a photo essay,' Tom said.

I liked the sound of that so much I used it as a subtitle. My project was called:

The Wetlands: My Favourite
Local Environment
A Photo Essay by Millie Childes

I remembered what Ms O'Grady had said about it being our own project and I wrote up special bits about why I personally liked the Wetlands and how living in this area had made me more aware of birds. I also wrote up a piece on

148.

how I took all the photos and even developed the black and white ones myself. I called this piece:

Technical Notes

In an exhibition catalogue Tom showed me there was also a section where the exhibiting photographers wrote their personal Mission Statements. That sounded good to me, but I didn't have a mission statement as a photographer yet. I thought I could do a mission statement about my environment instead.

Mission Statement

I'm concerned about my local environment and do my individual best to protect it and keep it the way it should be kept. I do not litter. My mother and I always recycle glass, plastic and paper. We re-use plastic bags. (I even have to take my lunch to school in old bread wrappers, which can be embarrassing.) We own a compost bin and a worm farm.

My mother believes that everyone should grow some of their own food. She says this gives us a connection with our environment. I personally grow cherry

149.

tomatoes, baby squash and lemon thyme.
It would be tragic if the Wetlands disappeared because we keep cutting down trees, using plastic bags and contributing to the greenhouse gases. Where would the pelicans, the herons and the moor hens live then? Our world would not be as wonderful a place without the birds, frogs, little fish and insects that live in these environments.

Only when I had finished all that could I look at the bird book. I thought about looking up 'bird with no neck' on Google, but Tom had said specifically the bird book and I didn't want to cheat.

The bird that flew over us in the dark was a rufous night heron. I found it by

(a) looking at wetlands birds

(b) checking out the pictures and trying to remember what our bird had looked like

(c) reading the descriptions.

I would have given up but I wanted to prove to Tom that I was up to the challenge. (I was also interested in what the special thing I was going to get was, but that wasn't the main reason. That was secondary. I really mean that. I thought the special thing was chocolate. It usually is.)

'It was probably a rufous night heron,' I told Tom triumphantly when he emerged from the darkroom. 'At least, that's what I think it was.'

'I think you're right,' he said, grinning, 'and I think this is a good photo. What do you reckon?'

It was a photo of me with Pavlov. We were mooching along by the lake's edge. I could remember Tom calling out to me and I'd turned around. That's when he took the photo. I was half turned to the camera. One half of my face was shielded by my hair, the other half was turned towards him. Pavlov had looked too. Behind us the lake was both busy with birds and still.

I looked at the photo. I wanted to tell him what I liked about it, the way Mum made me talk about her paintings, but it was a photo of me, so it was hard. He was watching me.

'I like it.'

'Why?'

'Okay, you have to know that when I'm talking about it, I'm not talking about a photo of me. Just a girl and her dog by some water. Is that a deal?'

'That's a deal.'

'What I like about the whole photo is that she's just an ordinary girl, the dog's a shaggy kind of ordinary dog. Nothing special is happening, you know? The girl's just turned around to look at someone who's called her, but …'

'Yes?'

'Well, it's special enough for someone to have

taken the photo in the first place, isn't it? So she must mean something to the person who is taking it. And so we look at her a bit harder, right? Isn't that the thing with photos?'

'Gee, Millie, sometimes I listen to you and I can just hear the fact that you are your mother's daughter.'

I was pleased, even though I was both my mother and my father's daughter, and myself, but of course Tom didn't know Patrick so he couldn't tell which parts were Patrick, which were Mum and which were just me.

'And your father's daughter,' Tom said, as though he could read my thoughts. 'That's how come you were so good in the darkroom and at procedure. The daughter of an artist and a scientist, and your own interesting self, Millie. What more could you need?'

I could think of a whole list of things I needed, but I knew what Tom meant so I stayed quiet.

'I owe you something special for the night heron,' he said, 'but I have to give this some thought, okay? So can you wait?'

'I didn't do it for that,' I said. 'I did it because I wanted to know.'

'I understand that. Listen, we'd better get home, because you still have to stick everything on your black card and Pavlov has to be fed.'

(Tom and I had eaten cold baked beans with hot toast. A gourmet delight, Tom said, depending on impact for the difference between the soft, cold, squishy texture of the baked beans and the hot, crunchy texture of the toast, but I knew what Mum would have said!)

When we got home it was after nine o'clock and the answering machine light was flashing like crazy.

'Oh dear,' Tom said, checking his watch, 'your mother had strict school-next-day bedtimes for you and already we've flouted them.'

'For a good cause. Do you mind if I go into your room and get the card?'

'Of course not. I'll play the messages.'

The first one was from Mum. My heart flip-flopped hearing her voice.

'Hi, Millie. Hi, Tom. Hope everything is okay and sorry to miss you both. Millie, I know something is happening this week at school. Hope you remember! Tom, dearest, another big thank you for stepping in like this and I do hope everything is okay. I'll try to ring later but there's an artists' dinner on so it might be quite late. If it's too late I won't, because you might be ... oops, there's the battery beep, I have to recharge. Miss you both and lots of love.'

I looked at Tom. He was smiling at the

answering machine in a particularly dopey fashion.

'Hi there, Kate, it's Sheri. I really need to talk to you. If you're there, pick up. Kate, pick up. So you're not there. Well, I don't know. Where else would you be? Kate, I need you.'

'Mum's best friend,' I said to Tom.

'Kate, it's Sheri. I rang before. I really need to talk to you. Pick up. Just pick up, Kate. I don't care what you're doing, stop it and pick up.'

'Kate, it's been hours and you haven't rung me or anything and my life is falling apart. Please call me, Kate, please. Mitchell and I need you. You and Millie. We need you both. Our life is falling … sorry, that should be past tense, our life has fallen apart. Ring us, Kate.'

'Something has happened,' I said. 'Something bad, Tom. Sheri wouldn't normally ring like that.'

'She sounds … well, I hesitate to say it, but she sounds a little melodramatic.'

'Are you going to ring her back?'

'I don't think I should.' Tom looked up and down the hallway as if there was someone else he could call upon. 'I don't even know her.'

'She sounds really sad, Tom, and Mum can't phone her. It's up to us.'

'I don't have the number.'

'It's in Mum's phone book. Here.'

'Look, Millie, I can't ring someone I don't know

and ask them why they're sad. You ring her.'

'Are you sure?'

'Well, you can tell her your mum's mobile battery is dead and you know her situation better than I do.'

'She hasn't got a situation,' I told him. 'She's just got a son called Mitchell and an ex-husband and she's living with this school counsellor called Brendan, who isn't particularly nice even though she loves him more than anything.'

'Sounds like a situation to me.'

'It's just Sheri,' I said. I was tired and wanted to go to bed and dream about being a world famous photographer. 'I'll ring, but you stand there, in case it's something you should talk to her about, okay?'

'It's a deal.' Tom actually moved one step forward and half a step towards me. 'How is that?'

'Perfect. It's ringing. It's still ringing. She's gone out, maybe … oh, no, oh, hold on. Shh. Hi, Sheri.'

Sheri sounded nearly hysterical.

'Kate,' she sobbed. 'Oh, Kate, thank heavens you rang. I've been ringing and ringing your number but it was always your blasted machine.'

'Sheri, it's Millie here, not Kate. Mum's in Sydney.'

'Millie, you sound just like your mother. Oh

Millie, I tried her mobile even – and he hates me making mobile calls. It's just that little message, "the person you are trying to contact," etc. I don't know who else to talk to. Have you got another number for her?'

'She's out,' I said. '*We* can't talk to her. She's out at an artists' dinner. Sheri, what's wrong? I can tell her when she rings next, if you like.'

'He was leading this double life, Millie. Brendan was. You know at Christmas when he took the presents to give to another family? A family in need, he said? They really were another family. His other family. Millie, I don't want to be telling you this. I'm so sorry.'

'She's sorry,' I mouthed at Tom.

'Who are you talking to?'

'Tom,' I said. 'You know, *The Boyfriend*. Sheri, do you want to talk to him? He's good with situations. He's very user-friendly.'

'There's nothing to do. Mitchell and I have to move out. I can't stand living here. I can't stand knowing he's seeing someone else, that he was always seeing someone else. It's just so …'

'Crappy,' I supplied for her. She seemed at a loss for words.

'Crappy.' Sheri laughed but it wasn't a good laugh, not a *gee, the world's a funny place* laugh. It was a laugh of doom. 'He used to get angry with me. Something Mitchell or I had done or hadn't done. Stupid things. Mitchell was always doing something wrong, according to Brendan. Leaving a tap dripping – he couldn't turn the taps hard enough. It was Brendan's fault, not changing the tap washers. But he'd get angry with Mitchell. He'd say, "How do you think we can save the world if kids like you don't become more responsible." I said to him, "You're a counsellor, Brendan. Do you think that's appropriate stuff to say to a seven-year-old?" "Well, Sheri," he'd say, "if you're not going to be responsible for the welfare of your child, someone has to be, I suppose." He'd say, "You don't make me feel very healthy, Sheri. I think I need to go somewhere else for a while", and then he'd get in his car and drive off. I'd sit there and cry, Millie. Brendan was feeling healthy somewhere else, yeah. He was feeling healthy with another woman.' There was a fresh wail of sobs.

'Look,' I said, 'I think you had better talk to Tom. He really helped with Rowan, you know.'

'Who is Rowan?'

'This boy I had a crush on. He went home to play snooker with Tayla who is the most horrible girl in the world.'

'What was Tom's advice?'

'Take-away pizza and videos,' I said promptly.

'Shall I put him on?'

'Oh, I may as well say hello,' Sheri said. 'Just hold on, I have to blow my nose.'

There was the squelchy hoot of a nose being blown and then Sheri came back on the phone.

'Thanks, Millie,' she said. 'You're a wonderful girl.'

I held out the phone receiver to Tom mutely. He looked at me with a pleading look but took it gingerly.

'Hello, Tom here … Yes, yes, that's right … Good, yes, very good. Actually she's seeing Patrick … No, I'm not worried … Well, okay, I was a little … at first … That's right, as you are with old … but I'm not now … That's terrible, Sheri … What a lying … Well, yes, I did say that … I was pretty young when take-away pizza worked, I must admit … Work, too, of course … No, I don't have any kids … I'm enjoying … Yes, she is … Yes, very … Oh, I think we're happy … very happy … I haven't met anyone quite … No … Well, no, you couldn't stay … Come here? … Well, I don't like …'

Sheri and Mitchell couldn't come here. I shook my head wildly at Tom. Not here, not with Mum away. I couldn't cope with them and neither could he. We weren't geared up for a heartbroken Sheri.

'There's not really any room,' Tom said firmly. 'And Kate isn't here. There must be somewhere else you can go, just for a couple of days? … Yes, I think that would be best … Please, don't think I'm … No … Well, that's right … I don't think we would … Good, I think that is a good idea … Back to Millie? Of course … And look, I think you're well out of it if he's seeing this other … All the time? Well, that is shocking … and with a child involved … just reprehensible … Maybe you should notify the school … Oh, I don't know … If you were calm … Well, it has to effect his professional … Sure, I understand that, but … Well, yes, he's in a position of telling others … It does sound as though he's abusing his … Perhaps it would be best to wait … Yes, Millie's here … Good talking to you, too, and I am so sorry, Sheri. It's a terrible thing he's done. He does sound like a complete … And from everything Kate and Millie have told me you're a wonderful … Oh, yes, here she is then. Bye.'

He held out the phone to me with a look of relief.

'Sheri? See I told you he was okay … Yes, she does seem very happy … I'm fine. We've been all afternoon in the darkroom, developing photographs … Give her a call tomorrow morning. I'll get you the number.' I read Mum's hotel number to Sheri. 'Okay. Yeah, Sheri, I love you too, lots and lots. Big hugs and to Mitchell, too … I think that's a good idea, Sheri. Your mum'll look after you for a couple of days and Mitchell loves her, too. Then Mum will be home. She'll know what to do ... Oh Sheri, of course I'd phone you ... Thank you. You take care, too. Let his stupid tyres down for me. Bye.'

'She's pretty upset,' Tom said, looking worried. 'You don't think she should have come here?'

'No.' I shook my head. Sheri upset was like a force of nature. You never knew what she'd do. 'She's going to her mother's place. Aunty Rox will look after her. She could even go to Mitchell's dad's place. He'd be happy to put them up, but she won't do that, of course. It could give him false hope.'

'Of course,' Tom said.

'You see what I mean about birds that mate for life,' I told him, yawning. 'It's a lot easier.'

Tom laughed. His laugh was a good laugh. It was that glad sound that tells the world you're happy with it.

'I think she's better out of it. What a ... well, what a dreadful man he must be.'

'Pig's Trotters, that's what I call him. His name is Trotter. Mum didn't like him from the start. She said he was controlling and ... a word beginning with g. Glib. She said he was glib. What does glib mean?'

'Someone who says a lot of stuff, you know, talks the talk but it is all talk and no substance. He sounds worse than that, though.'

'Oh, I'm sure Mum will find a few new things to say about him now. Sheri will be okay, though. She's pretty cool and tough in her own way.'

'You know, Millie, not all men are like that. I wouldn't ever …'

'You're cool, too.' I punched him lightly on his shoulder. 'I don't think you need to worry.'

'Thanks, Millie. Bed now, okay? I'll set the alarm for a bit early tomorrow morning and we can do the photographs then. You won't be able to see straight if you stay up any longer.'

I yawned a yawn wide enough to swallow a cat. 'Nup, you're right. Okay. See you in the morning.'

Before I went to sleep though I made a curse against Brendan Trotter. It's not that I believe in them, necessarily, but it felt good to do it for Sheri. I put it in my journal. I didn't call on the Spirit of everything Fair and Just this time, just whatever spirits were out there listening. Here's what I wrote:

The Curses on Pig's Trotters
      aka Brendan J. Trotter

Make Brendan Trotter miss Sheri every miserable moment of his days and his other woman leave him, too, in disgust at the
    feeble, shallow person he is. Make his

clients give him a book titled 'Twelve Steps to Being a Successful Human' because he so clearly isn't. Make his toilet plumbing go wrong. Make his stupid counselling books go mouldy and his car rust. Give him tyre punctures, flat batteries and nothing but static on his radio. Make him ring Sheri up begging for forgiveness and have her hang up in his ear. Make his own mother tell him he's a disappointment to the human race. Let him know every day how horribly and disgustingly he's behaved and let him regret it every single day he wakes up.

And then, just to even things up, I put in a good wish for Sheri, because either one could work, then.

Wish for Sheri
aka Kate Childes' best friend in the world
and Millie Childes honorary other-mother

I wish that Sheri would find a proper Boyfriend who knows and obeys the Boyfriend rules of good behaviour and who is so delighted to have someone as talented and funny as Sheri in his life that he

never fights with her but just loves her, in
a strong and real way the way everyone
deserves.

CHAPTER THIRTEEN

Ms O'Grady was in a fluster the next day at school.

'Projects,' she said, 'projects everyone. Come on, we've got very important visitors today. I want all the projects displayed. It's politician time.'

She cracked the whip all first period. We begged more map pins and display boards from other classrooms, we laid unmountable projects on desks and begged a laptop from the computer lab so Erin's power point could be displayed to full effect.

The politician came through at the end of second period. We had to chorus out 'Good morning, Ms Connors', and listen while she gave a short talk about why she became a politician and what she cared about. Then we had to go and stand next to our projects while she walked around the room with the principal and asked us questions about them.

'This is excellent work,' she said peering at mine. 'Did you really take the photographs?'

'Yes,' I said, 'and I developed them myself with my mother's boyfriend. He's a photographer, you see.'

'Fantastic, and such a good message too. Well done … Millie, is it?'

Then she passed on, leaving a sniff of lovely perfume behind her. I was pleased she'd picked me out. She didn't stop at everyone's projects. I suppose she didn't have time to do that.

'Well done, everyone,' Ms O'Grady said, after the principal and the politician had left. 'You were terrific. Ms Connors was impressed. In fact she was so impressed with the projects that she's donated a couple of prizes for the best students. Ms Farn will present them tomorrow at assembly, but I'm going to tell you now who got the prizes so you can make sure you're wearing assembly-appropriate uniforms and so you can invite your parents, if they're free. Millie Childes, Sarah Reed and Nate Redfern, congratulations!'

Sarah squealed and hugged me, as though we'd just won an Olympic medal or something.

'What do we get Ms?' Nate asked, when the class had stopped clapping. 'What's the prize?'

'I don't know. Probably a book or something like that,' Ms O'Grady said. 'But Nate, it's the honour, not the prize.'

After that we all toured around the room looking at each other's projects. I paid attention to Rowan's sport and the environment project. It was sloppy. His smile didn't seem to make my knees tremble any more, and he kept combing his gelled hair with his fingers as though the little spiked bits would flop over if he didn't check them all the time. His skin wasn't too hot, either. I know I shouldn't talk (Miss Pimple Queen of the Universe), but I didn't have them clustered on my forehead in little crusty clumps.

I was over Rowan. He wasn't my type.

Funny how you can decide that kind of thing and the other person can just have no idea.

Helen-Sarah-Rachel-and-I were sitting around at lunchtime when Rowan came up.

'Hey, Millie,' he said, 'those photographs were awesome. What happened to you at basketball? I looked everywhere but you'd just disappeared. Would you like to come again on Saturday? And bring your camera? It'd be great to get some shots of the game.'

I could hear Helen-Sarah-and-Rachel hold their breaths. I looked at Rowan and smiled.

'How was Tayla's new pool table?' I asked him sweetly.

'Pretty good. Her dad bought us Maccas for lunch. It was cool. But Millie, I could take you to Maccas next Saturday. I've got some pocket money.'

'I'm sorry, Rowan, I'm just not into action photography. I prefer landscape and portrait shots. They've got more depth, you know. They're more of a challenge, really. Action shots are kind of point and hope. So thanks but no thanks, if you know what I mean.'

His face was interesting. First he looked confused, then he looked stunned and finally he looked sulky.

'Tayla's right,' he said. 'You are stuck up.' And he walked away.

'You dumped him,' Rachel said. 'I don't believe it, Millie Childes. You dumped Rowan!'

'I didn't dump him exactly.' My stomach was all weird but at the same time I felt I could breathe more easily. I sat up straighter. 'I just don't want to waste my Saturdays photographing some dumb basketball game. Anyway, I don't really have a camera. I used one of Tom's.'

'Doesn't matter,' Helen said. 'You really did dump him. That was the coolest thing I've heard.'

It was all round the school by the end of the day.

Tom was at home when I got home and I told him the whole story, starting with the politician and ending with the accidental dumping.

'So you'll have to come to assembly tomorrow morning. Can you, Tom? Because Mum won't be there and Nate said his mum will definitely go and both Sarah's parents are probably going to be there because they're on late shifts this week. Could you come, please?'

'Well, well,' Tom said, 'this is unexpected. Yes, I suppose I could. I don't teach until tomorrow afternoon. I could be there. You don't think the school will think it a bit ... you know ... unusual?'

'Of course not. This is the twenty-first century, Tom, not the Dark Ages.'

'Right. It's a date, Millie. Here, I got something for you, too – my part of our deal.' He handed me a largish square box and then stepped back to watch me unwrap it.

Inside was a camera case and inside the camera case was a 35 mm camera. The same one I had already used.

'It's really a spare,' Tom said quickly. 'It isn't new or anything. I hope you don't mind, but it is a good one and you can get extra lenses for it.

There's a zoom lens in the case for you already, but you might eventually like to get a wide-angle or a portrait lens, depending on how interested you become. I thought about a digital camera but I think that could wait. They're obviously the way of the future and there are some fine photographers having lots of fun with them and producing some wonderful stuff, but really with me with a darkroom and, you did seem to enjoy the enlarging process ... This way, I thought, you could find out about it all the old way, which does give you the best grounding ... and, Millie, I hope you like it. Is it okay?'

'Oh Tom,' I said, 'it's just the best present ever. Thank you so much, thank you.' I wanted to hug him but it wasn't Christmas so I didn't feel I could. 'Honestly, it's just ... magic.' And I hoped he knew that I would have given him a hug if it had been Christmas or even my birthday.

Tom made that little chuckly sound. 'Well, well,' he said, 'it will be good, eh? There's a local camera club you might like to join too. Of course, most of the members would be a bit older than you, but I know a couple of kids who are keen, too. They turn up with their parents and do their own thing.'

That night Mum rang and I was able to tell her everything, from Sheri to the project. Then I gave

Tom the phone and I went into my bedroom to look at my camera again and to give him some privacy. He was on the phone for ages, but it must have been okay, because he was all smiley and happy when he came out.

'I told your mum I'd pick her up at the airport,' he said. 'She gets in on Thursday at about three o'clock. She said you'd be fine on your own after school.'

'Can't I come?' I asked. 'I love airports.'

'You'll be at school.'

'I could miss it for a day,' I said. 'I'm doing okay and Thursday we have sport anyway, practically all day.'

'I don't know, Millie, missing school is missing school. I'll have to ask your mother.'

'If you didn't ask her, it would be a surprise. That would be pretty good, don't you think?'

'I'll have to think about this, Millie.'

The assembly was nerve-wracking. I didn't expect to be nervous. At my old school we had to go up all the time in assembly and get awards – student of the week, best help with the preppies, neatest work for the week – but there weren't as many people watching you and there wasn't a stage either.

Sarah, Nate and I had to wait until all the announcements were made and then Ms Farn called us forward.

'We were lucky enough to have a visit yesterday from our local member of parliament, Ms Connor, who was so impressed with the projects done by Ms O'Grady's Grade 7.1 that she personally selected three of the students to receive awards for their work.

Grade 7.1 did projects on "My Environment" and Ms Connor said of the work of these three students that it was — and I'm quoting from an email she sent this morning — "original, inspiring and thoughtful". Congratulations to Millie Childes, Sarah Reed and Nate Redfern. Please step forward, students, to receive your generous book vouchers donated by Ms Connor herself.'

We had to file onto the stage, one by one, shake Ms Farn's hand, get an envelope and then go off the stage again. My knees were shaking but it was good, too.

'Twenty-five dollars!' Nate said, ripping open his envelope. 'Gee, that's more than I got for my birthday. Pretty good prize, eh?'

I looked at Nate. It was interesting that a boy was so excited by a book voucher.

'What will you get, Millie?' he asked.

'A book on photography,' I said. 'That's what I'll get. Tom gave me a camera last night, a camera of my very own. A Pentax 35 mm.'

'How come you got that?'

'For answering a question about a bird,' I said. 'But I think I really got it because I'm interested in photography.'

'You're into birds, too, aren't you?'

'I like them. What are you into?'

'Bashing around the bush. I do that a bit. Mum and I belong to a bushwalking club. I do a bit of fishing, too, sometimes. Mum and I like that. You have to be very quiet. We go camping, too. We read a lot.'

'Sounds like the kind of thing my mum and I do,' I said, 'except we aren't bushwalkers.'

'Well, we're not particularly serious bushwalkers. We don't do overnight hikes. Although Mum reckons we could if we wanted. I like to get out, look around. You know.'

I did know what he meant. It sounded like it could be fun. You could certainly take a camera on a bushwalk. I thought I might mention it to Tom.

'Can anyone …' I started to say, just as Nate said, 'Maybe you'd like …' and we both apologised.

Then Tom came up and the moment got lost. But that was okay, too, because Nate wasn't the kind of boy, I didn't think, to let a moment go forever or become distracted by a mobile phone game. Someone who fished couldn't afford to get easily distracted.

That night I enlarged a photograph of Tom to give to Mum as a present. Then we picked a couple and made them sepia-coloured, rather than black and white, which made them look old.

'What are you giving Mum?' I asked Tom.

'Do you think I should get her something?'

'No,' I said, 'she won't expect it or anything. I'm just giving her the photo because … well, it's really the first time she's been away by herself for simply ages. And I want to surprise her. That's all.'

'I'd like to, too. What do you reckon she'd like?'

'Flowers are always good.'

'No, if I'm going to get a present, I want a proper Kate present.'

'Earrings, then. She loves earrings.'

'Gee, I don't know, Millie. Earrings are kind of difficult.'

'You wanted a Kate-present.'

'I did, but I didn't expect earrings to be the answer.'

'Well, she wears them all the time,' I told him. 'She loves them, and Patrick has been the only other man to ever give them to her.'

Tom looked at me and rolled his eyes. 'That's supposed to inspire me with confidence?'

I shrugged. 'Patrick's a scientist,' I said, 'and you're a photographer. I would have thought earrings would have been more a photographer thing than a scientist thing, but Patrick managed.'

'Okay, here's the deal — you come shopping with me for Kate's earrings tomorrow morning and you can come to the airport with me. What do you say?'

'You're on! And can we get a photography book with my voucher, too?'

In the end I needed Tom's help more than he needed mine. He found Kate-earrings really easily. I had a hard job deciding between the photography books but Tom found the one he recommended to his students so I used the voucher to put it on lay-by. It was the first time I'd put anything on lay-by and I was a bit worried I might lose the docket, but the woman behind the counter said it would be fine even if I did, because they had their own record.

'I'm taking my camera to the airport,' I told Tom. 'I want to get a photo of Mum when she sees us.'

'That's a good idea. I take a camera almost everywhere, Millie. You never know what you might see.'

I think people at the airport thought Mum was some kind of celebrity. Tom and I both took photos of her as she came through the gate. I took more while she and Tom kissed, which they did for so long I had time to focus properly. I would have felt really embarrassed by them hugging and kissing without my camera. The camera made me think of things other than *Oh-my-goodness-that's-my-mum-kissing-The-Boyfriend-at-the-airport-with-everyone-watching-them-I-could-just-die.* The camera made me think, *Wow! I like it that I can't really see their faces. Then they become just two people at the airport, rather than Mum and Tom.* And, *Ooh, now I can see a bit of Mum's face over his shoulder and I like the way her hand is on his back like that.*

We had a snack at the airport, which turned out to be a good thing. When we got home the first thing we saw was a rainbow-coloured Kombi van parked outside our house. There was a bright wreath of plastic flowers hanging on the tow bar and the number plate read 'So funky', which was also painted on the side.

'Oh my goodness!' Mum practically shouted, 'it's Sheri!'

There they were, Sheri and Mitchell, sitting on our front doorstep.

'You look gorgeous,' Sheri said to Mum. 'You look fantastic. Life here must suit you. I'm thinking of moving. I looked the TAFE up on the Net. They actually teach Textile Design. I'm a textile artist,' she explained to Tom, who was looking confused, 'and I could just hang around and do some markets while I waited for an opening. No, Kate, don't look alarmed. I won't be moving in. Just hanging around. My heart's broken, that shameless rotter, so there's nothing left for us back in Graystone. We might as well move to where our real family is – that's what we thought, wasn't it, Mitchell?'

'I didn't ever want to leave you guys,' Mitchell whispered to me. 'I didn't like the way Brendan smiled with all his teeth but his eyes never crinkled up, you know, the way they should.'

'I'll never look at another man,' Sheri declared.

'Go on, Sheri, just because Brendan Trotter was …'

'A complete loser. Sorry kids, but that's the truth. I'm focusing on my career now. I'm going to expand my range. Do you like the van? I got it cheap. Mitchell helped paint it. I'm going to take up screen printing. It's amazing what you can do with screen-printed fabric. Kate, you and Millie can be my walking advertisements. I might even do some men's shirts, very groovy subversive ones, screen-printed. Tom, how would you feel about wearing 'So funky's' new line of shirts around town?'

'I'd be honoured,' Tom said, which was exactly

the right thing to say and Mum, Sheri and I all beamed at him.

'He's a keeper,' Sheri said, 'unlike Brendan, who was a loser. And, Mitchell, I don't mean that in the way you kids at school use the word. I mean he was someone I needed to lose. I think this deserves champagne. Now Kate, I know you've just got back from Sydney or wherever you were, so what I suggest is that we all toast to Life and Recovery from Twelve Step Programs and then Mitchell and I will stay here tonight with Millie and you and Tom can go off and be romantic at his place.'

'Well,' Mum said, looking helpless, 'I don't know.'

'It's a great idea,' Tom said and got a further smile from Sheri.

'I think this could be our kind of town,' she said. 'Not too far from Mitchell's dad, a fresh start for us, but most importantly back with Kate and Millie, our family — oh, and Tom, too, of course.'

'A toast to the families you make,' Mum said. 'And welcome home, Sheri.'

After Mum and Tom left, Mitchell and I made up a bed for him in the study.

'You're lucky,' Mitchell said, putting a pillowcase on the pillow, 'Tom's eyes really crinkle. Hey, do you know what Mum did to Pig's Trotter?

177.

She went into his office, at home, you know, where he kept all his stuff – client reports and accounts and everything – and she pulled everything out and put it back all wrong.'

'I rearranged things for him,' Sheri said, appearing at the door. 'It was a mean and horrible thing to do but he deserved it. I was particularly messy with his accounts. It will take him days to sort it all out and it's GST time looming, which he hated anyway. I'm not normally into revenge, but honestly, Millie, he was such a lying user. I had to do something, otherwise my rage would have spilled over and on to the innocent. '

'You just broke into his office?'

'It wasn't locked so I didn't break in.'

'Couldn't he call in the police?'

'What, and say that the woman he was living with and cheating on had rearranged all his personal files so he couldn't find anything? He'd look too big a fool.'

'She went around to the other woman's house, too,' Mitchell said. 'She was awesome.'

'She had to know,' Sheri said calmly. 'I just told her exactly what Brendan had been saying and promising to me. Turned out he'd been saying the same things to her. She didn't take it too well, either.'

'I wish I had seen you do it.' I said.

'Oh no, baby.' Sheri hugged me. She smelled of roses and vanilla. She always did. It was a completely different scent to the one Mum wore but just as swoony. 'I don't think you want to see that kind of thing. Better that you see people loving and respectful of each other, the way your mum and Tom are together. That's what you should be seeing, not the wild acts of wronged women.'

'That's such a cool thing to say, Sheri – it's like poetry. The wild acts of wronged women. Do you mind if I write that down in my journal?'

My brand new journal was very thick and had a great cover, red with bright polka spots all over it. Inside it Mum had drawn a funny picture of me and underneath it she had written:

To Millie, hoping that the entries in this book are filled with joy and delight. Please note that I bought an unlined book, because I thought you might like to stick some photos in, too, now that you are a photographer.
lots of love, Mum.

I hadn't thought of photographs, not in my journal. But I could see what she meant. It was a brand new book, waiting just for me.

I both love and hate that moment when you begin to write in a new journal. This book felt

179.

almost too beautiful to write in. I found my best pen. It was an actual fountain pen Mum had used when she was around my age. It even had her name engraved along the side, in silver.

I wanted to do something really special in my new journal, something that would make the person who read it in the future say to themselves, 'What a girl that Millie must have been'.

So on the first page I wrote a heading: 'Things I've Learnt This Year', and then I sucked the end of the pen for a little while thinking, before I started writing my most important list to date:

1. It's useful to see how a person smiles. Mitchell is right - all teeth and no eye-crinkles is shallow and phony.

2. You do make families, and mine can only get bigger, just as it has this year with Tom and Helen-and-Sarah-and-Rachel, who might not all stay in it forever the way Sheri and Mum have but are there for the next little while anyway.

3. You can get over your heart breaking.

4. The wild acts of wronged women might

help but ...

5. It still hurts like billyo - and it is better
 to be a kookaburra and mate for life,
   no matter what Tom says.

6. I, Millie Childes, am an individual and
    although I get it wrong sometimes
    (see references to Rowan, previously
    known as *R.H.* in my earlier journal),
     I also get it right sometimes.

7. When you look at the world from behind
    a camera lens you see it a little
   differently, as though it is already
     framed somehow and really pieces of
    light and shade ... which, when you think
     about it, might not be a bad way to
     look at the world.